In Paris With You

Clémentine Beauvais

Translated from the French
by Sam Taylor

90 YEARS OF EXCELLENCE
FABER & FABER

528 712 88 X

Freely inspired by

Alexander Pushkin's verse novel

Eugene Onegin *(1837)*

and Pyotr Ilyich Tchaikovsky's opera

Eugene Onegin *(1879)*

First published in France in 2016 by Sarbacane under the title *Songe à la Douceur*
First published in the UK in 2018 by Faber & Faber Limited
Bloomsbury House, 74–77 Great Russell Street, London, WC1B 3DA
This paperback edition first published in 2019

Typeset by MRules
Printed by CPI Group (UK) Ltd, Croydon CR0 4YY
All rights reserved
© Clémentine Beauvais, 2016
English translation © Sam Taylor, 2018
'In Paris With You' on p.v from *Yellow Tulips* © James Fenton
Published and reprinted by permission of Faber & Faber

The right of Clémentine Beauvais to be identified as author of this work
has been asserted in accordance with Section 77 of the Copyright,
Designs and Patents Act 1988

A CIP record for this book
is available from the British Library

ISBN 978–0–571–33972–3

10 9 8 7 6 5 4 3 2 1

Don't talk to me of love. Let's talk of Paris,
The little bit of Paris in our view.
There's that crack across the ceiling
And the hotel walls are peeling
And I'm in Paris with you.

James Fenton, 'In Paris With You'

1

Because their story didn't end at the right time, in the
right place,
    because they let their feelings go to waste,
it was written, I think, that Eugene and Tatiana
    would find each other
    ten years later,
    one morning in winter,
    under terra firma,
on the Meteor, Line 14 (magenta) of the
                    Paris
                       Metro.
It was quarter to nine.
    Imagine Eugene, dressed up fine: black corduroys,
    pale blue check Oxford shirt, sensible collar, charcoal
    tweed jacket, a grey scarf,
probably cashmere, frayed at the ends,

wrapped once,
twice
around his neck – and above this hung a face
that had softened
since the last time;
a face written more loosely,
a face less harsh, and more   patient.
Suppler, gentler.
A face rinsed clean of its adolescence;
the face of a young man
who had learned to stifle his impatience,
a young man who had learned how to wait.

Tatiana, funnily enough,
had been thinking about him the previous evening.
Which might seem an amazing coincidence,
except that she often thought about him
– and I'm sure that
you, too, can brood and mope,
sometimes, about love affairs
that went wrong years ago.
The pain's not worse after ten years.
It doesn't necessarily increase with time.
It's not

an investment,

you know,

regret.

Lost love doesn't have to be a tragedy.

There's not always enough material there for a story.

But for these two,

I'll make an exception, if you don't mind.

Look how shaken they are to find

each other again.

Look at their eyes . . .

'Eugene, hi, haven't seen you for ages!'

beamed Tatiana, a pretty good actress.

He sat down next to her; the seat was still warm.

On the black window reflecting his face,

a sleeper's forehead had stamped

a little circle of grease

like the watermark on a banknote.

A record of time spent,   now disappearing.

Tatiana could see herself in the window too,

at an angle, as the train sped up, roaring.

The sudden surges, sharp bends and screeching stops of

Line 14 are notoriously vicious. It's hard to stand up or chat

or read. But it does have an upside: it takes you from your

first stop
    to your last
        fast.

    As they rushed from one place to another,
Tatiana stared at the window that reflected him and her
together.

        Eugene yelled:

            'So how are things? I had no idea
            you were pregnant . . .'

    She wasn't.
And yet, it was difficult to contradict Eugene at that
moment, since on her duffle coat was a massive badge, and
on that badge a baby grinned, a big white speech bubble
proudly declaring in capital letters:

BABY ON BOARD!

And in smaller letters, just below:

        THANK YOU FOR GIVING ME YOUR SEAT.

    So it was only logical that Eugene
(who was feeling somewhat upset by this news,
and surprised to be upset, and a bit confused)
    should come to this conclusion.

4

There was an explanation,
which could not be given then and there:
            that because empty seats were so rare
            on the Paris metro between eight
            and nine a.m.,
    Tatiana had, a few months before,
bought this VIP (very impregnated person) pass,
            her guarantee of a place to rest her bum.
            She loved seeing all those kind
            ladies and gentlemen
            spot her badge and leap to their feet
            as if their seat
            were on fire.
            She would thank them, flashing
            soft Virgin Mary smiles.
And since there was nothing secret about her condition,
it often set off shouted conversations
about baby names,

                and baby clothes,
and giving birth,   and epidurals,
                and nurseries,
            and breastfeeding,
and so on,   and so on.
She'd had to do some research into the mysteries of

maternity.

> She needed a coherent story,
> for at that time of day, it was often the same
> passengers standing/swaying/sitting
> in the train carriage.
> She couldn't claim one day that she was
> four months gone with twins,
> and the next that it was a little girl with Down's
> that she and her husband had decided to keep,
> and the day after *that* that it was
> a miracle child, conceived after eight rounds of IVF,
> and the day after *that* that she was
> a surrogate mother for two gay men.

No one would believe her if her story kept changing.
This need for precision was the price she had to pay
for a free seat every day ...   until spring,
when she could ride a Vélib' to the National Library
without shivering.

> 'Who's the father?' asked Eugene.
> 'The father? His name's Murray.'
> 'Murray? Do I know him?'
> 'No, I don't think so – he's British,'
> said Tatiana, who had just invented him.

6

For a moment they were silent.
Then Tatiana paid him a compliment:

'You look very elegant!'

'Ah, thank you,' Eugene replied.

'I'm going to my grandfather's funeral.'

'Oh! That's great!' said Tatiana,

who obviously hadn't given herself
enough time to process this information.

Next station:
Gare de Lyon.

To the right, on the other side of
the tracks, a lush tropical forest suddenly appeared
behind glass.

(I remember how,

aged seven or eight,

I used to daydream

about seeing snakes

and monkeys in there.)

The doors slid open and a voice, automated,

intimated

in three languages, no less,

that passengers should exit from the left side of the train.

Bajada por el lado izquierdo.

(When I was young and everything
was new and a source of wonder,
I used to ponder
what kind of aliens this obscure message was addressing.
'It's in case there are any Spaniards on the train,'
my father explained.
'So they know where to get off.'
I wasn't sure what Spaniards were.
I imagined them tall and rubbery,
I don't know why.
For months,
whenever we came into the Gare de Lyon, I would watch,
heart pounding, hands clasping my skirt, eager
for a glimpse of those elastic creatures,
who,
disobeying the train man's very clear directive,
would open the door jungle side and vanish, undetected,
into the forest of palms.)

*****

But let's get back to our two passengers.
Their memories are more important than mine.
They have things to tell each other that they can't articulate.

So they say other stuff, though of course it barely conceals
      what's really on their minds.
One of those cowardly conversations,
         on this and that and the weather,
         avoiding the heart of the matter.
That's what happens when everything has gone to waste:
we can't say it out loud;
we chicken out.
Thankfully someone inside us speaks in our place.

         'So what about you? Where are you going?'
Eugene asked politely.
         'To the National Library. Like I do
         every morning,
                  at precisely
                  the same time ... you know,
if by any chance you're planning to make the same trip
tomorrow ...'
         He's going to the cemetery, you idiot!
Tatiana yelled at herself inside her head.
                                    Thankfully,
it was fine:
Eugene didn't notice her blunder,
busy as he was trying to remember

what he was supposed to be doing
tomorrow at quarter to nine.

        'What are you up to in the library?'

        'I'm working on my thesis.

        I'm in the last year of my PhD.'

        'Oh yeah? What's your thesis about?'

        'History of art. It's on Caillebotte.

        Gustave Caillebotte.'

        Then she shifted into autopilot:

Don't worry, no one knows anything about Caillebotte . . .

'Don't worry, no one knows anything about Caillebotte. He was a nineteenth-century artist – a painter and collector, theoretically part of the Impressionist movement, but in fact his paintings are much more precise, more classical in a way – you might have seen one of his more famous pictures: a view of Paris in the rain, Haussmann-style buildings like a ship's bow, with a man and a woman under an umbrella . . .'

        'I know,

        I know,'

        Eugene interrupted.

        'I know exactly who Caillebotte is,' he muttered.

        'Ah! Perfect.

        Well then, you know everything.'

To her chagrin, Tatiana felt that this declaration
somehow carried the implication
that her thesis didn't really

                              amount to much.
Not wishing to leave Eugene with this impression,
she started to describe to him,
        with a level of detail
        that might seem excessive,
        part of her third chapter,
        still largely hypothetical at this stage,
        about the representation of water
        in Caillebotte's art; in this chapter,
        Tatiana demonstrated,
        in a boldly rhetorical way,
        that the liquid elements
        in Caillebotte's paintings
                – rivers, bathwater, rain –
        were a sort of discreet reply
        to the stodgy, spongy daubings
        of certain other artists
        around at the same time.

                        *****

When she finished this explanation,
the train howled to a stop
at the National Library metro station.
Eugene got off too.

'Is your funeral near here?' asked Tatiana,
not very tactfully.

'It's at the Kremlin-Bicêtre cemetery.
I'm going to walk. I have plenty of time.'
They stood in silence on the escalator,

Tatiana leaning clumsily to the right,
turned backwards
so she could face Eugene,
her right foot in front of her left
to hide the ladder
in her tights.

Eugene seemed pensive.
Tatiana noticed
some fine lines on his brow
that had not been there last time,
though she might have anticipated their arrival
because of all the frowning he used to do ten years ago
to express his disapproval.

As a teen he'd disapproved of everything –
the boy was always bored –
while she'd been too easily pleased
and lost in a daydream.
She wondered vaguely if she was still in love with him.

'It'd be nice to see each other again,' Eugene told her
halfway up the escalator.

As this sentence prompted a thousand questions,
Tatiana asked none of them
and concentrated instead
on the immediate perils of her ascension:
her left arm,
     pulled by the handrail,
          was escaping upwards,
                    faster
                         than the steps.
She checked that her scarf was not dragging on the floor,
to make sure it wouldn't choke her at the end of the ride.
(She'd seen a video of a similar incident
on the Internet.

                    The guy died.)

'Can I have your number?' Eugene asked.

'Of course,' she said, reciting it digit by digit.

He texted her so she would have his too.

She already had it.

Apparently he hadn't changed his number
in the past ten years.

Apparently he hadn't kept hers.

'How's Olga?' Eugene asked casually,

as they were elbowing their way towards the
turnstiles.

'Oh . . . fine, you know. She's got two daughters now.'

'Ah, cool! They'll be cousins to yours, I mean.'

Tatiana had momentarily forgotten the whole story with
the badge.

This was her chance to come clean:

'Listen, I'm not really pregnant. I just bought this
thing

so I'd get a seat on the metro every morning.'

Eugene threw his head back and laughed.

But the laughter surprised him
because it was more than laughter.

It gave Eugene the feeling
that he was

like a snowdrop or something,
one of those flowers that break
through the white winter crust
            and suddenly breathe the icy air.
        The laughter of someone who, until that laugh,
                must not have been truly aware
                that he was alive.
'I did think you were a bit young for that kind of
responsibility.'

        'People always feel too young for responsibility,'
said Tatiana. 'Any kind.

        A kitten, a bonsai tree . . .

                        Keeping your ticket
                        till the end of your journey.'
        She sighed as if to herself. 'I have to use tickets now.
I didn't renew my Navigo card – I've got no murray at the
moment.'

        'No murray?'

                'No money.

                        Damn it,
        I don't know why
                I can't speak properly today.'
'But no Murray either?' Eugene ventured.
'No Murray either, no. Murray

was an underground invention.'
Eugene smiled and nodded, alarmed at the realisation
  that the mere
  idea
  of brushing against Tatiana – the crowd was pressed
tight together as everyone pushed towards the exit –
  made his head swim,
      knees buckle
          and pulse race
              as though
  he were standing on the top of a high-dive board
  staring into the depths
                              below.
    'You go first, it'll be easier that way.'
  The turnstile must have had a sense of humour
(or maybe it was just that their wool coats rubbed against
each other)
because it gave them an electric shock.

  Tatiana stuck her ticket in an ikebana of trash,
a foul efflorescence of ash,
in one of those bins where smokers stub their cigarettes.

  Outside, it was the usual tornado

between the four towers of the National Library.
    In all kinds of weather,
    even in the middle of a hot August afternoon,
    while the whole city languishes, breathlessly,
    under a coal-black sun,
those library stairways are eternally swept by typhoons.
Apparently it's an aerodynamic phenomenon
related to the positioning
of the towers.
A small architectural mistake.
        And everyone complains about it, everyone bellyaches,
                            but no one thinks of the joy
                                of those four buildings
                                    playing ping-
                                pong with the wind,
                                    lifting up skirts,
                    artistically swirling the leaves and dirt.
                                        It's too bad
            how the happiness of some makes others sad.

    Eugene and Tatiana walked through this whirlwind,
    and between them brief electrifying glances
    darted and fled,
        the way little crabs dart and flee

when children touch their fingers
to a rock pool by the sea.
Their little dance of glances
might have gone on like this forever,
but someone got in the way.
He was a tall man,
　　　handsome,
　　　　　　perhaps,
if your idea of beauty is the cold hard
ice of marble, if your idea of beauty
is the tough leather, scarred,
of tree bark.
He was a powerful man,
　　　sensual,
　　　　　　perhaps,
if sensuality for you
is a craggy mountaintop
in the wind-lashed dawn.
I believe it was Edmund Burke who used the word *sublime*
　　　to describe that beauty, cracked and mineral,
　　　that wild beauty, rough and material,
　　　which not only attracts but terrifies.
　　　'How glad I am to see you, Tatiana!
　　　I'd wondered if our paths might cross today,'

declared this man, who was, it turned out,
the supervisor of her thesis on Caillebotte.
She hastened to introduce him to Eugene,
who caught only brief snatches of their words,

Mr Leprince
well-known specialist
French Impressionism

preoccupied as he was by other things:

made notable discoveries
about Renoir

Tatiana's pink, chapped lips, her dimpled chin,
a few white cat hairs on her raspberry scarf,
her posture, curved to the left

was the curator
of the exhibition at the
Musée du Luxembourg

by the weight of her bag,
presumably stuffed with books and notes.
'That's very interesting,' said Eugene,
who really couldn't have cared less about Caillebotte
or Renoir
or Monet

and analysed
Degas's correspondence

or Degas.

    Bloody Degas,

with his stupid ballerinas.

But just to participate in the conversation, he said: 'Hey,
that reminds me – it's been ages since I went to the Musée
d'Orsay.'

    It was then that Eugene noticed Tatiana's dark

        shining hair,

    blown by the wind

into delicate arcs.

        And what, my dear,

        are your plans for the day?

    He also noticed that she had very pretty teeth,

    small, pearly, with nice little spaces –

he hadn't realised that back then.

        Hang on,

didn't she used to wear braces

before?

    Before: ten years ago, she was ... Hang on ...

Fourteen!

Well yeah, there you go: fourteen.

At that age, you're still under construction.

        I'm going to reread Valéry

        as you suggested recently

And now, it had all changed: her hair, her skin, her teeth.
I remember how young she seemed,
 like a little kid.

> *I didn't take enough notes before.*
> *And it's always useful to return*
> *to sources that you think you know.*

And I was practically an adult, thought Eugene.

 And suddenly
he remembered: fuck, I was seventeen. Seventeen!
 Seventeen years old! Christ, that's beyond belief.
Did it really exist, that age? Seventeen!
 It's impossible, seventeen. It's pure fiction.
 It's an age dreamed up to make old people believe
 that they used to be adolescents.
 Whereas in reality, it's absolutely certain
 that no one in the whole wide world
 was ever seventeen.
Eugene, however, was beginning to realise

> *If you ever need to see me,*
> *just drop by*

 that this thesis supervisor, sublime
 in the Burkean sense of the term,
 was, quite calmly and casually,

your brilliant work

is always a pleasure to read

but very clearly, trying to pull Tatiana.

It was obvious that he, too, had seen

the interlacing of her hair in the wind,

her white teeth, those nice spaces in between,

and I am of course eager

to hear you speak

at the museum

next week

and he suddenly wondered if there wasn't something
going on between those two

that he should

have been told about,

before remembering that, only this morning,

as recently as quarter to nine,

he hadn't thought about Tatiana more than five or
six times

in ten years.

He'd tried his best not to; whenever he'd got close,
anywhere near,

to thinking of her, by chance – of her, of that summer –

he'd tiptoed back,

clicked shut the door,

again and again,

on that room in his mind where he'd stored

that July, that August, those joys. That pain.

So she'd been wiped from his memory for years,

and now here he was, full of fears,

like some jealous husband,

a member of the Taliban,

some big macho idiot: the kind of guy who appears on

TV at one

in the morning

to explain why he can't stand the fact that his wife is

a fan of Simon Le Bon.

And yet it was interesting for Eugene, who had hardly ever

experienced this kind of feeling before,

to sense the overwhelming power of his desire,

when he looked at this man (sublime

in the Burkean sense of the term),

to murder him

in a very aggressive way.

by the by, I heard that a wonderful article you wrote

is going to be published in Art History?

Eugene was overcome by the urge to provoke him

to a duel,

like they used to in the olden days.

If Lensky was here, he'd have been his second.

Shit, he hadn't thought about Lensky in years!

I've really got to go, I've booked
a desk in the library for half past nine.

It was Tatiana who'd said those words.

Until soon, maybe, Eugene . . .

Tatiana was leaving. She'd booked
a desk for half past nine.

The library awaits!

The library awaited.

It was nice to see you again.
Really nice.

It was nice. Really nice.

A kiss on the left cheek, a kiss on the right cheek.

The smell of cold,

cigarettes, bergamot.

Time to get back to my Caillebotte.

What a stupid name, Caillebotte. Really, it was the
stupidest name ever.

He watched

with wonder

Tatiana

descend

the stairs

in the gusts

of the architectural blunder.

As Eugene was about to leave, feeling a bit flat,
tired and sad,

the sublime (in the Burkean sense of the term) man
suddenly said

in his guttural voice –

the kind of voice you hear on posh radio stations
like France Culture;

a voice drowning in static; rough, gravelly,

the kind you want to sweep like a driveway –
he said in this voice to Eugene:
'And how is it, sir, that you know Tatiana?
I don't believe she has mentioned your name.'

'I was friends with the boyfriend of her Olga sister,'
replied Eugene, forcing himself to use the same
rhythm, but getting his words mixed up.

'I mean, her older sister. Olga,' he corrected.
'Ah! A genuine, longstanding connection!
Then I'm not telling you anything new if I say
That she is the brightest student in my collection;
From the indistinct mass of my PhDs,

She emerges, like a beam cast on the sea
By a lighthouse, its dazzling reflection,
Or the little firefly hovering softly
In the dark night; incandescent perfection . . .'
    'What the hell is he on about?' thought Eugene.
    'This is a public declaration of love!

        Live from the steps of the National Library!
    He might just as well

               yell
very very loudly   through a megaphone:
  I love Tatiana! I love Tatiana! I love Tatiana!
Is he mad or what? Why tell me that?
    Oh, this is torture.'
And he stood still as stone,
    stunned by the truth of this idea.
'The bastard.

    He is torturing me.'
The man droned on in his voice from France Culture:
'I had forgotten all about the pleasures of the mind
And was calmly drifting to the end of my career
When Tatiana appeared and magically undermined
The daily trudge and drear . . .'

           'Lensky was a poet,'
           Eugene thought.

'But not this kind of poet.

Not like this pompous Leprince.

Is he sleeping with her?'

At nine thirty-five in the morning, logically,

this question should not have entered his head.

But now it was

the most important question in the world.

The key question.

'Is he sleeping with her?'

Eugene discovered that he had other questions too.

Hundreds of thousands of questions,

which he asked himself feverishly

while Leprince did his worst,

spouting declarations of love in rhyming verse.

She didn't ask me what I did for a living – doesn't she care

is she still angry

with me

who could blame her after what I said

is she sleeping with him

how

in whose bed

what exactly did I tell her

I can't even remember now

dear Tatiana

no, not even a *dear* I don't think I even said *dear*
I was a little turd back then
        I was hardly even me back then
   has she thought about me recently
did she recognise me straight away
        why has she changed like that
        has she really changed
        as much as all that
was she that pretty before
was she that witty before
was it the brace on her teeth that hid her soul from me
   is thirty-five minutes enough time
   to fall in love with a girl
or fall back in love
        was I in love with her   back then
        did I have a personality   back then
        was I really a human being   back then
        was there anything inside my head
is he sleeping with her
is he sleeping with her?
        I don't remember what I told her that day
     if only I could remember
                what the hell did I say?

then I could explain

        perhaps she's waiting for me to apologise
      but I could hardly apologise to her just then
      down in the metro, on the fourteenth line,
      five minutes after seeing her again
am I getting myself worked up

              over nothing very much
      did she already possess such beauty
      such intelligence such personality
        is she sleeping with him
would anyone notice if
I missed my grandfather's funeral?

      yeah
      probably
I think Mum would probably notice
particularly as I'm supposed to give a speech
      damn
      if I run
         could I catch her
     is she already in the library
     is she waiting for me to call her
        is he sleeping with her
        is he sleeping with her?

These are just some
of the thousands of questions
that we will leave Eugene (for now) to wrestle
with, alone.

Because it's time
for a brief summary of the facts.
It's time to go back
about ten years
into the past,

back to when it all began.

2

It all began

        in a leafy suburb of Paris,

        neither poor nor very rich,

        in a white house

        that looks like a Playmobil house.

There, Tatiana lives peacefully

with her older sister Olga

and their mother.

The fourth actor in this domestic tragedy

                    (not counting me)

is the neighbours' son.

His real name is Léonard,

though everyone calls him Lensky.

He's a poet,

        but not the boring sort.

He does slam – like rap, but slower.

Like poetry, but with music.

The kind of poetry that adults don't consider poetic.

Gosh, Léonard, it's not exactly Rimbaud, is it,
what you do? It's not exactly Keats.

Our son is a sort of rapper.

It's not exactly poetry. We're hoping one day he
might broaden his vocabulary.

And lose the hip-hop beats.

'It's just a phase,' the neighbour bleats.

So Lensky does slam that's neither Rimbaud
nor Keats.

He's also sleeping with Olga
and they love each other.

They're seventeen. Lensky pens
wild declarations of love to his girlfriend.

I've kept every single one, because I like them so much.

They make me smile.

But that's not all.

What those letters have
is that sweet shame of things
we used to find beautiful,
that sour aftertaste of words we regret
years later.

Those overblown oaths,

those preposterous promises, those demented declarations,
          those metaphors that afterwards make us groan,
     that overheated hyperbole, those ridiculous repetitions
which somehow, in the heat of the moment, struck us as so
beautiful, so true,
our pens dipped in the ink of our souls,
our entire beings calligraphed into those curls,
the whole universe
          concentrated in the verse
whispered by the lips
of our beloved muse,
as they read our immortal prose somewhere,
rolling our Rs, licking our Ls, wallowing in our Ws . . .
It seemed to us that we were nothing more
          nor less
     than their warm breath:
the sculpture of our words on their tongues, in their air.
          'I love you, Olga, I love you so!'
          (So begin most
          of Lensky's letters.)
          'I love you like the moonstruck madman
          loves his lunacy.
Every hour, every minute, every second, you are all I see.
As I stare out from my rooftop at the city far below, your

sweet visage smiles back at me from clouds and sun and snow. Ever since that blessed day when your eyes first met mine . . .'

(Despite his parents' concerns, there is nothing wrong with his vocabulary. Parents often underestimate their children. Even more so their teenagers. Lensky, in fact, has read Rimbaud.)

'. . . across the garden wall, when we were small, our souls have been entwined. You are the essence of my existence. You are my greatest experience. I live you like a poet thinks. I live you like an alcoholic drinks. I love you, I love you, Olga, and I would rather die than live a day without you in my life.'

He sends these lines on paper in the post,
in emails, instant messages, and texts
(though not so often, because texts
are extremely expensive in 2006),
and he whispers them into her ear,
on the pillow they share,

the two of them naked,
lying in bed,

skin touching skin,
their bellies still scaly with bodily fluids,
their chests still heaving in the muggy gloom
of Olga's little attic room.

Meanwhile in her bed on the floor below,
fourteen-year-old
Tatiana
reads,   reads,
reads,   reads,   reads,   reads,   reads,
reads,   reads,
reads
books by the Brontë sisters, Jane Austen, Zola,
Boris Vian, Aragon and Shakespeare:

Pride and Prejudice,
Wuthering Heights,
Froth on the Daydream,
Gone With the Wind,
Romeo and Juliet,
The Ladies' Paradise
(etc.)

and as she reads,
she imagines wild, passionate, heart-stopping love affairs.
Or so I like to think, at least.

35

Tatiana is a very old-fashioned young girl.
I imagine her imagining a rather surly heart-throb,
        dark-eyed, rough, even cruel to start with;
        the kind of man who's been through things
        that no young girl can even imagine.
Encountering Tatiana, however,
            this bull of a man,
            transfixed by her beauty and her virtue,
            experiences a pulsating, life-changing love
            which will of course be thwarted by various
incidents
and events.

    For example:
    One time, she might be kidnapped by the mafia (or
some sort of hoodlums anyway) – in the shape of three
very bad (but not bad-looking) men,
        who want to dig up dirt
        on her mystery man,
        because he's working as a spy for their enemy
(or something);
so they threaten to hurt
            Tatiana,
                to torture her, even,
                    unless

she confesses

everything she knows about him!

(Though in fact it's not the kind of torture

that would actually hurt her:

electrical wires that aren't plugged in;

ropes not tied so tightly that they burn her skin;

her torturer too susceptible to her beauty

to really do his duty.)

And suddenly one of the gangsters will stop

and stare

and shout in a panicked voice:

Who's there?

And she will be saved in the nick of time

by the man who loves her,

and they will walk off hand in hand into the sunset

to be wed,

but,

inevitably,

he will already be married!

(An arranged marriage, obviously,

as never, before Tatiana, will he ever have loved anyone

else at all.

Ever.

Tatiana will be his first.)

And his first wife, who is still alive
(and whom he hates, naturally)
                will return and try to kill
                them both –
                                but she won't succeed. Because
            Tatiana's husband will protect her, holding off his
            wretched wife easily at first, but then, distracted by his
            overwhelming love for Tatiana, he will be stabbed in the
            back and he'll start to bleed profusely; Tatiana, courageous
            and cunning, will bring down a chandelier on the woman's
                head, before fashioning a tourniquet for her wounded
                husband with a strip of cloth torn from her dress.

Filled with admiration, her husband will tell her
over and over again how much he loves her.

                        There are, of course, upon this theme,
                    an almost infinite number of variations.
                        Tatiana does not lack imagination.

At the Alexander-Pushkin Secondary School,
where she goes every day,
            Tatiana finds nobody worthy of her love.
Obviously,

since the boys are all fools.

God they're stupid those boys

they're all so dumb

they're really annoying

they pinch our bums

they're so immature　　　　　*they fart*

and they snigger

idiotically　　　*they talk about*

whose willy is bigger　　　*and that*

is all they think about　　*those pathetic prats*

The girls talk about how boys change

when their balls descend.

Apparently, that hasn't yet happened.

anyway everyone knows that girls are more intelligent.

*****

But one day

everything changes.

One day, Eugene arrives in the leafy suburb.

Where does he come from?

Eugene is from a wealthy background,

a family　　　based in Paris

but who are aristocratic,

originally   from the North,
conservative and Catholic.

Eugene is the youngest; he has three older sisters.
He's been to several private schools.
He's not what anyone would call

                                        a good student,
        even if he 'has the ability', as people say:
        in other words, his parents still pray
that one day he will pull his bloody finger out
(to quote his impatient father),
that he will discover the value
of hard work and deep thought
(in the words of his more refined mother),
and that he will pass his Baccalaureate exam, then ascend
to higher education.

                An icy silence is Eugene's only reaction.
                He feels lost, in the age of the smiley;
                Heir to a bitter, old-fashioned melancholy.
                Everything bores him; there's no consolation
                In his arid desolation.

He's done all the stuff he's supposed to, of course –
Smoking, sleeping around, drinking, drugs, or worse.

He's painted, he's written, he's roamed the whole planet,
But nothing gave him any real pleasure, damn it!
At night, on the verge of sleep, Eugene often
Imagines it all ending with the implosion of the sun.
Since everything one day will be this vast absence,
Why bother trying to give meaning to existence?
Why expend such futile effort, why get annoyed,
When everything is doomed to end up in the void?
How stupid they are, those idiots who strain
Themselves by working or trying to entertain
Others or themselves, who seek pleasure and delight,
Just to distract their minds from the impending night!
At seventeen, Eugene knows all about the world:
And as life is so pointless, he does nothing at all.

    The summer before his final year of school,
in the depths of boredom,

                    Eugene considers his options:
  • kill himself
  • stay with Lensky for the holidays
After due
     mature reflection,
     he chooses

              option number two.

Lensky is his only friend, kind of.

He met him first on a forum and then in real life.

Eugene likes Lensky because they're
like brothers:

both live at a distance
from the world of others.

Lensky lives metaphorically. He doesn't care
about things; he dares

to love madly,

to transcend the ordinary,

to create his own world of drama and poetry.

He's a wild-eyed optimist, a daydream believer.

In Lensky, Eugene sees himself flipped
like a reflection in a mirror.

So in early July, Eugene tells his parents,

in their apartment

in the eighth arrondissement,

that he's made an important decision:

he's going to spend the summer with Lensky
and not in a coffin.

His mother, sitting on a blue
Louis XVI chair, can only nod
her approval of this choice.

Living in the suburbs,

though not without its faults,

is generally preferable to lying dead in a vault.

And as he seems in a good mood,

she decides to add:

'I bought some past exam papers

for business school; you can pack them in your bag.'

Arriving at Lensky's place, Eugene quickly notes

that his friend now has only one thing on his mind;

one word, obsessive and grandiose:

Olga Olga Olga Olga Olga Olga Olga Olga Olga Olga Olga

And even though Eugene thinks all love is dumb,

he adores seeing Lensky so possessed by this girl.

It thrills him to think that one day the sun

will implode, swallowing up the world

and everything in it – including this reason-defying love,

this love as pure as dreaming,

as bright as a window's reflection.

For Eugene, this thought is

perfection.

For him, it's the ultimate proof

of the absolute insignificance of being.

*****

The day after Eugene arrives, Lensky persuades
              him to go next door to meet Olga,
                   because he's sure they'll get on well,
              and most of all because
              he wants to hear him say
              that she is the most beautiful, intelligent girl
              in the known universe
              (and also because he hasn't slept with her
              for two whole days
              and he feels like his balls are about to burst).
              Eugene is not
              expecting much from this meeting,
              but then he never expects
                   anything much of anything.
For Lensky's sake, he composes a socially acceptable
expression,
puts on a pair of 501s, white Converse trainers,
thin-rimmed tortoiseshell glasses.
              Stifling a yawn,
                   he follows his friend out onto the lawn.
              In the garden next door, Olga and Tatiana await
unseen.
Tatiana's nose, as ever, is buried in a book.
Olga: split skirt, sandals, magazine.

'*Mesdames*,' Lensky bows, with a look

of pride, then kisses Olga's hand

and Tatiana's cheek,

before introducing them to Eugene, who claims he is enchanted

to meet

them both. 'Enchanted, truly,' he lies,

this boy who has never been enchanted

by anything in his life,

and certainly not by the mundane sight

of two suburban teenagers in their garden,

sipping Coca-Cola,

crossing and uncrossing their long slender thighs

to the background hum

of buzzing bees

in a honeysuckle mountain

that crowns a wooden pergola.

All this too will be swallowed by the sun.

As Lensky recites his latest poem to Olga in a

corner of the lawn

('I love you from dawn till dusk,

from dusk till dawn!'),

Eugene feels compelled by the rules of decorum

to talk to Tatiana, who would have been perfectly content
to continue reading.

    'What you reading?' Eugene enquires.
It's *La princesse de Clèves*, one of the most
    boring books ever written
    in Eugene's opinion.
'I haven't read it,' he claims. 'What's the story?'
Studious Tatiana, who has read the book ten times,
gives him a passionate account of the plot,
with its unconsummated romance

    ('*That's true, I'd forgotten,*' Eugene recalls.

    '*They don't even get in each other's pants.*')
between the Princess of Clèves and the Duke of Nemours.
After listening to this for ten minutes –

    and it wasn't such a chore,
in fact, when he thinks about it –
Eugene decides it is his turn to entertain the young lady, so
he begins
to tell her about his life, employing all his charm
and skill at conversation,
with his number one weapon:
the power of exaggeration.

    'I've just come from Paris,
    where my uncle kicked the bucket.'

'Oh, that's awful! I'm so sorry,'
says Tatiana, who's easily impressed.
'Oh, don't worry,'
says Eugene. 'Fuck it –
we needed the rest.
We'd spent months plumping his damn pillows and
bringing him cup after cup
of lapsang souchong tea –
it smells like smoked salmon,
you know the one I mean?
The guy was the CEO of an oil company,
responsible for a dozen spills at sea.
So he killed entire families of seagulls and penguins and
other sea creatures, most of them probably very cute!
Seals, Tatiana, baby seals! This guy strangled baby seals
with his own bare hands! Surely you can see
that it's wrong to mourn the passing of someone who spent
his time plotting the death of cute aquatic creatures?
And because he was so bloody despotic,
he forced all his cousins,
nephews, nieces and grandchildren
to visit him
during his death throes (which dragged on
for a frankly inconvenient length of time)

and be really kind and nice and all that crap,
even though he'd been such a bastard
all his life.
This is a man, Tatiana, who gave me a sponge bag
for my ninth birthday.
                    A check, sand-coloured sponge bag.
What kind of sick jerk does something like that?'

Hearing these words, Tatiana's emotions are divided
                    between
        horror   and   fascination
            but she quickly opts for the second
            of these sensations,
            which has the advantage of being
            the same thing she feels
        when her gaze dwells
on Eugene's rugged face,
                those precipitous cheekbones, that abrupt
nose,
that lopsided smile, those
                beautiful eyes
so blue . . .   Russian blue,
Tatiana decides;
the blue of Russian palaces on pillows of snow.

48

She notices the way he crosses his legs,
right calf resting on left knee, and how
he has forearms in the shape of triangles;
the boys she knows at school

God they're stupid those boys

have forearms thin as Pringles,
forearms that might snap if they tried to lift a heavy tool.

they're all so dumb

And his hands, with their knotty ligaments and veins,
not like the soft round hands of the boys she knows

they've got no brains

those rubbery little hands, that doughy skin;
Eugene's hands are models of power and precision,
hands that let you see their structure, their mechanism.
And those wiry veins bulge and pulse from within
the muscles of his hands, his arms, his neck.

(And I think at this point, it isn't too hasty
to say that Tatiana is in love already.)

She and Eugene continue to chat about this and that
while Lensky does whatever he's doing with Olga;
and Tatiana, who adores his presence near her
and wants him to stay there forever,

is at the same time eager for him to leave;

she can't wait

to lock herself in her room, alone,

giddy with emotion,

to lean her hot forehead on the cold windowpane,

free at last to imagine herself with Eugene.

Which is paradoxical, because right now he *is* with her.

But she wants him to leave, so she can be with him better.

Finally the two lovers return,

Lensky relaxed and smiling,

Olga warm and pink,

both calm and quiet, sedated by their love.

While they pour themselves lashings of Coke,

Tatiana thinks

to ask Eugene if he's on MSN.

He gives her his address,

though the idea that she will write to him

makes him want to spew.

'Hi Eugene, its Tatiana, how r u? ☺'

Smileys make Eugene cringe,

those pathetic pixelated phony feelings,

those insipid idiotic infantile emotions;

he has to remind himself that one day,

they, too, will be swallowed by the sun.
        But he has a recurring nightmare
        where, with tragic irony,
        those brainless heads with their dumb
        smiling lips,
        sole survivors of the Apocalypse,
        float through a liquid plasma universe
        laughing or crying or blushing into infinity.
But Eugene has no reason to worry:
Tatiana has no intention of chatting with him,
        least of all on MSN;
        the address is merely an accessory,
        a prop for her theatre of the mind,
        intended to decorate a corner
        of her cosy dream
                where she could,
                        if she wanted,
spend all night talking with Eugene,
and where he would be happy to talk with her too.
        The address makes her fantasy feel real
        but with no actual obligation to do
        anything at all.

*****

And so, in a frenzy of impatience,
Tatiana goes back into the house;
there are still

      four hours

          before bedtime.

    At dinner, Olga too is miles away;
she's thinking

    about Lensky, who's gone for the evening,
    about the afternoon they spent together,
    but most of all about the texts she's sent him,
and whether

    he will ever reply to any of them, ever.
She knows he's going out in Paris with Eugene tonight.
Maybe – *maybe* – he hasn't received her texts because
there's no reception on the train?

    She should give him the benefit of the doubt,
she thinks;
And yet

    it is almost more probable, for Olga,
    that he's already with another girl,
    for example in the toilets of a bar
    or out on the street, up against a wall,
    or in some seedy hotel in Pigalle.
    Olga has a whole battery of imaginary adulteries

to hand

       and has no trouble hearing
the creaks and moans, picturing the multiple positions
of the two of them –   or three,
      if that's the kind of thing he likes, Lensky.
It's been an hour and ten minutes since she sent her last
message –

             Hey babe what r u doing?

– and Olga is starting to think that, by now,
it would be better
      if she heard on the evening news
            that he'd been killed
            in a train crash
            or blown up by terrorists.
So Olga's jealousy flashes up scenes both sleazy and morbid
(she will find out later that he left his phone at home)
      while Tatiana, for her part, turning pale
as she holds back a diarrhoea of daydreams,
is waiting for just one thing: to be in bed.

      Spare a thought here for the girls' poor mum,
      trying to make conversation with the two of them.

*****

Meanwhile,

       on the train that's taking them

       to the Gare du Nord,

Lensky tells Eugene all about Olga,

but his friend says hardly anything at all

       of any consequence,

       even drifting into a bored silence,

as if he found the subject of Lensky's beloved quite banal:

       Unable to stand this anymore,

       Lensky says at last:

       'So . . . so come on,

    tell me   mate,

come on, tell me,   what

    do you think of her, huh?

           Olga,

I mean . . .   I mean I know it's not really your thing,

girls and all that . . .   I know you've given up on . . .

    [chuckle]   matters of the heart,

      but   seriously

   mate,

    tell me, what do you think of Olga?'

Eugene's mind swings like a pendulum.

He really likes Lensky   but also the truth, you see.

The first demands compassion   the second, honesty.

To start with, he thinks he'll just say something weak:

'Olga? She's nice.

Yeah, mate, she's really nice and that.'

'And that? Don't you think she's beautiful?'

'She's ... honestly, she's fine.'

She's got her legs in the right place.

Two eyes and one nose on her face.

There's nothing wrong with her,

as far as I can see.

Eugene hates himself a little

for being incapable of hypocrisy.

Lensky fiddles with the wheel of his iPod Mini.

'But, you know,' says Eugene,

'I didn't really talk to her.

I spent most of the afternoon with Tatiana.'

'That's true,' mutters Lensky.

'You got lumbered with her sister. I'm sorry.

I should have let you talk to Olga more,

then you'd have seen ...

you'd understand ...'

'Don't apologise,'

replies Eugene. 'Really, I mean it.'

And he sounds like he really does,
this time.

'Honestly, it wasn't bad at all. She's actually fine,
Tatiana.

I mean, honestly, if I were you,
I don't know
which of the two sisters I would choose.'

Silence, then the train wheels
squeal.

Inaudible announcement: a suspicious package
or an incident on the line.

Lensky frowns as he disentangles
the wires, entwined,
of his earphones.

Eugene suddenly remembers the 'compassion' side
of his inner pendulum:

'But hang on,
mate, I mean,
I'm not saying you made the wrong choice.

I'm just saying
that Tatiana   is, you know,   *all right.*'

As Eugene digs and digs with his spade of words,

the hole growing ever deeper,

    the sides plunging ever steeper,

Lensky lapses into a cold silence

that lasts until his second mojito, one hour later,

    when at last the rum, the sugar,

    the mint and the lime,

    the crushed ice,

    revive his generous, loving, joyous,

    seventeen-year-old poet's soul.

    He remembers what exactly it is about Eugene

    that he likes:

this is a boy who says what he thinks.

    Who cares if he doesn't love Olga?

    Lensky loves her and that's all that counts.

    So they dance,

and Lensky slaps his friend on the back

    as Eugene moves on the dancefloor,

daiquiri in hand:

he dances well enough,

not Michael Jackson, but nothing to be ashamed of;

he dances the way he might

tell some old aunt about his holidays:

conscientiously, but without passion.

(In the years that follow,
in rare moments of reflection
about himself, and Lensky, and the two girls
next door,
about that fateful summer
when everything was ruined,

Eugene will sometimes recall that silence
on the train to Paris,
Lensky's stiff expression,
Plasticine skin,
his gaze coiled
in the twisting wires
of his headphones,
lost in the music within.

With hindsight, that silence will seem
to Eugene like a warning,
a foreshadowing
                        of doom,
as in a tragedy of old;
a brief chill heralding the long dark winter cold.)

This is known as tragic irony. I am pointing it out here
                        so you will appreciate just how neatly
                                    this story is tied together;

how completely
reality mirrors the laws of fiction.
I can say this without fear
of being thought immodest, since this story
is not my invention.
As for the hows and whys of this wintry silence,
of this fountain that will soon run dry,
of Lensky's eternal fade to grey . . .
well, we'll come back to that.
For the moment,
Lensky is happy,
Eugene distant,
and Olga and Tatiana think about them
as they pick at their rillettes.
So everything is fine, more or less.

*****

The summer drifts on, and the boys
visit the girls in their garden almost every day.

For an hour each afternoon,
Lensky and Olga sneak up to her attic room,
and Eugene is stuck with Tatiana.

Which is not necessarily a bad thing,
since Eugene thinks she is –
allow me to remind you –
all right.
So he makes himself presentable,
and as he is perfectly capable
of being thoroughly charming

> when he wants to,
> and as he wants to
> quite often
> when he's with Tatiana,

for her, those afternoon visits are like
the visits of a magical, sensual being,
as if it were a prince or a centaur she were seeing.
The hour always follows the same pattern:

The forged-iron garden gate

> creaks
> > on its hinges;

Olga uncrosses her long thighs,

> slender and sleek,
> shades her eyes with her fingers;

Lensky arrives first, and the four of them
talk about the weather

until Lensky and Olga go upstairs because
        she has something funny to show him.
So Tatiana is forced to abandon
        her fantasies of Eugene
        and make do with Eugene
        in person.

        They sit in the gossamer shade of a tree
                and talk. That's all.
        About literature, cinema, music, poetry,
but most of all about the world in general,
and their feelings about it,
a little bit.
        Their first conversations are clumsy,
Tatiana flaky, Eugene overbearing,
the two of them stumbling, interrupting each other,
not
    But   quite   *I think*   yet   *No go on*
    No no you were saying   *Oh all I was saying was*
                able to speak in sync,
Eugene always wanting to say more,   Tatiana less;
she a flute,
he a bassoon,
he booming above,

she whispering below:
at first they talk at cross-purposes,
but soon,
little by little, as in a game of pick-up sticks,
with infinite precaution,
the two of them learn
                    to lift, one by one,
                              taking turns,
their frail criss-crossing ideas,
              sharp and light,
                                        sometimes confused,
              and some fall off and roll away,
              while others get caught,
              and some of them they use
              to pick up other thoughts.
Little by little, too, they each learn to anticipate
the other's foibles. Tatiana watches out for the double
dimples
              that bookend Eugene's lips like quotation marks
              whenever he cites a line of poetry
              or some captivating phrase

Summer's lease hath all too short a date   I will show
you fear in a handful of dust   Life is what happens to

you while you are busy making other plans   More than
kisses, letters mingle souls   The child,
a monster that adults fashion from their regrets

Eugene knows dozens of such quotations; the diligence of a
wax memory, stamped by everything that touches it;
generally, he uses this ability to shine in society,
        but with Tatiana, it's different; what he likes,
when he reels off lines,
        is not the idea of impressing her,
        it's not that . . .   it's
        the way she takes the time to think
        about the meaning of the quotes,
the way she picks them up and examines them,
these thoughts
which he hands to her still in their shell,
        till, freshly peeled,
she hands them back again, their fruit revealed.

Whenever Tatiana thinks out loud, she has a strange habit
of placing an insect on the back of her hand;
        a ladybird, a beetle, an ant:
                any bug will do.
Mechanically, she grabs some passing creature by chance

63

and as she speaks, fully focused on her words,
she watches it crawl from hand to hand, from skin to skin.
Eugene watches Tatiana watch the insect and wonders
about the meaning of this miniature marathon,

> the tickling of those tiny feet;
> perhaps somehow that stubborn,
> relentless linear charge,
> that furious forward march
> helps her to trace the path of her own thoughts?
> Her thoughts,
> they're not the thoughts of someone who believes
> that the sun will implode.
> Her mind is full of hopes
> and fears;

Eugene likes the jolting way she expresses her ideas.

*But like you see the other day my aunt told me
I should enjoy my youth while it lasts and I don't know
about you but personally I find that a bit artificial it
makes me kind of anxious in fact I think it's impossible
to deliberately set out to enjoy something it just happens
on its own and it's only afterwards later on that I think to
myself that moment was important for me because in the
moment itself I'm not concentrating on it being important
because that would make me anxious*

you know what I mean?

Nothing has made Eugene anxious

for quite some time,

and nothing has given him enjoyment either,

but, for one reason or another,

he's reluctant to disillusion Tatiana,

to tell her that her worries are a waste of time,

that her dreams are mirages:

out of kindness,

he lets her believe that all this stuff matters.

Once, only once, does he let the truth come out,

when she asks him the question:

'What would you like to do when you're older?'

This question irritates him; he replies that he couldn't care

less, there's nothing special he wants to do.

'When I'm older, I'll feel just as bored and down

as I do now.'

Tatiana is shocked. 'But Eugene, surely you want,

I don't know,

to do something that excites you or makes you feel

fulfilled?'

'There's nothing I like.'

'Nothing?'

'Nothing?'   Tatiana's face falls.

'Nothing.'

Even chatting with me? she wonders,

    not daring to ask the question out loud:

        Are you bored,

        sitting here with me now?

'But ... talking with   people,

or travelling the world ...'

Eugene snaps. 'Boredom exists everywhere, you know.

        It's called different things.

        We say *ennui*, the English *spleen*,

        the Russians *khandra*.

        But changing the name doesn't alter the feeling.

You can't escape your mind.

        Boredom is not a place you can just leave behind.'

        Tatiana had no idea

    about this terrible void inside Eugene.

        Up to this point, he had kept it unseen.

She falls silent.   Does this mean that he's depressed?

                Suicidal?

    She's heard about people who see the world in grey.

    Does this mean that   all this time

with her

he's been stifling yawns every day?
Eugene watches the worry on her face,
and is touched,   a little bit,
that she's worried about him, and curiously he feels a
twinge of guilt,
which is not an emotion he's accustomed to.
He softens his voice, makes a joke or two,
tells her that he would actually like to travel,
to see the Tierra del Fuego
(total bullshit),

but that he doesn't know what he wants to do
for a job when he's older;
his parents are always bugging him about that
and that's why he got annoyed
(crappy excuse),
but of course he's not always bored
(of course he is)   here, for example, now,
he's not unhappy, he's fine.   Yes he is.
'*Khandra* cannot enter through that gate.'
'I've been spleen-free since I arrived here.'
'This garden banishes boredom.'
Tatiana is relieved, she smiles again,
and ironically Eugene almost believes his own lie,

in the end,

        whether he changed his mind, alone,
        or Tatiana's happiness infected him;
so maybe, in the end, it's simply true:
        in this garden, you can't feel blue.

And so with the passing days,
        Tatiana in a rosy haze
of love, Eugene, a little amazed,
finds her increasingly
charming . . .
well, original anyway,   you know, not dull.
Disarming.
He wonders how
this Playmobil house could have produced
one girl full of dreams and ideals,
fiercely intelligent, sharp and delicate as a needle,
        and another whose Myspace page
        is decorated with a photo of Audrey Hepburn
        in *Breakfast at Tiffany's*,
        a reference that is probably, in her estimation,
        the very height of sophistication.

Eugene is not unhappy to spend his afternoons

with Tatiana.

No,   he is far from unhappy.

Tatiana, on the other hand, is so exhausted
        by these brief visits,
        when he sits
        with her in the garden,
and the dreams that rack her
        before and after
leave her heart and abs so sore and stiff,
        that she feels like she's in training
        for the Olympics.
Her programme of palpitations is packed to the limit:
    • All morning, she thinks about Eugene.
            At this stage, it's mostly in little bits;
she remembers his wrist, his ankle, his nails.
A Eugene jigsaw.
Each piece makes her heart contract, as if trapped between
a tiny finger and thumb.
    • In the afternoon, she thinks about Eugene.
            At any moment now, he might arrive;
her heart pounds so hard it makes the trees shake,
her throat aches – then –
    • Then he arrives.

Now she is obliged to think about him
while he sits there right in front of her,
which maddens her senses, this superimposition of Eugenes,
                    and Tatiana is all internal tension,
                    infernal desire, frantic for him to go away,
                    desperate for him to stay.
    • And in the evening, she thinks about Eugene.
Now her thoughts bloom fantastically; in the dark,
everything is worse – bouncing ball in her belly, skin cold
and damp as a fish's scales, forehead hot as lava, and an
army of pale hairs stand to attention on her arms.
        Her thoughts are like a Hollywood film.
        On the black screen of her white nights,
        Tatiana, still a little naïve, keeps fading to black:
at the moment when Eugene unclips her bra
                            fade to black
at the moment when Eugene's lips brush her collar bone
                            fade to black
at the moment when Eugene unbuttons his jeans
                            fade to black
We always fade in again
                    the next morning,
                    when Tatiana is fully clothed,
                    when they are eating breakfast together,

when they're chatting in the garden, united
by the knowledge that something's happened
                              and no one knows.

                    black/white/black/white
                black/white/black/white/black/white

            One can only admire it, this innate self-censorship,
            this discipline within;
but despite the chastity of her dreams, Tatiana still doesn't
fall asleep until dawn.
                And when she sleeps, she thrashes about,
                and when she wakes, she feels like
                she's spent the whole night fighting her covers,
                which are wrapped tight around her
                like an octopus.
And these thoughts barely have time to stagnate:
                every day, they are refreshed by something new.
Something Eugene's said,
a lock of hair he's put back in place,
the arm of his glasses that he sucked, deep in thought,
the hint of a hesitation on his face;
                Tatiana hoards all these little Eugene treasures
                in the storeroom of her dreams, a shop

where she is the sole customer,
the sole vendor.

hello madam I would like to buy
the little mole from Eugene's neck please   yes that one
yes yes the one that looks like a peppercorn
                    thank you kindly
it's to decorate my daydream where I kiss him just there
you see
          would you by any chance have a jar
              of his favourite expressions?
                 that's right
          I'm planning an imaginary conversation
                 with him tonight

Sometimes these treasures prove explosive, intoxicating,
a detail marked with DANGER;
                    let's say, for example,
that one afternoon he took her hand
in order to look at her watch,
then, that evening:
I'd like a copy
of the sensation of his two fingers on my wrist.
                                    Oh dear!

Are you sure?

Absolutely.

       You know this guarantees you won't fall asleep
           until three or three-thirty in the morning!

I know, but I need it.

         I should warn you, it's highly addictive.

I'll be careful with it.

                  All right.

            If you say so. But please follow
                  the instructions.

I will, I promise. Thank you.

The most dangerous of these treasures
gets delivered to Tatiana on the day that changes her life.

That day, while deep in conversation,
as she's explaining something

     very interesting

about butterflies at the time of the Industrial Revolution,

     the world is suddenly torn apart:

Eugene takes off his sweater, and his polo shirt is lifted
up –

          and

          she

          sees

a

fine

dark

line

of

hairs

running like a pencil shading

from his navel to his belt buckle.

And then beyond.

Down to where?

down to his   damn

she was in the middle of explaining

something very interesting

about something

white butterflies   no, they were black   no, hang on

in England during the Industrial Revolution

the butterflies were white

but, you see, there was lots of soot,

she tells Eugene   because of the factories

the butterflies were white, before   but then, because

of the soot   oh God, where

was I?   oh yes, so   to clarify

so it was the time of the Industrial Revolution in England

are you with me so far?

'I'm with you so far,' Eugene smiles.

And so, in fact   it was   it was all dark   I mean

oh I can't explain it

'It was all dark because of the smoke from the factories,'

encourages Eugene.

The fine dark line of hairs has disappeared again

under the polo shirt

but it remains imprinted

on her retina,

seared to her poor stunned brain.

'Yes,' says Tatiana, 'that's right,

so in fact –   *concentrate*   – the walls of

London were white before, and so were the butterflies,

but when the walls became black because of the soot, the

butterflies evolved and they became black too.'

bravo Tatiana, she congratulates herself,

that was a more or less coherent explanation

now get thee behind me, fine dark line,

come back tonight when I'll need you

as a prop for my dreams

'It's proof that a dark world

makes you dark,' concludes Eugene.

'Yes,' stammers Tatiana. 'I mean, no,

it's actually proof of Darwin's theory, so ...
I mean, don't you think it's amazing, that
whole thing about white butterflies becoming black?'

Eugene laughs.　　　'I don't know
　　　　　　　　about the butterflies, but you
　　　　　　　　are bright red, suddenly.'

　　　　　　　And indeed our poor Tatiana is vermilion.
　　　　　　　　　Like those little butterflies,
　　　she would like to disappear at the end of the garden
　　　　　(and I too must admit that I find it surprising
　　　　　　that we so want to blend into the background,
　　　　　　　　that we wish to vanish into the door,
　　　　　　　　　the wallpaper, the carpet on the floor,
　　　　　and that so often this chameleon desire arrives
　　　　　　at the very moment when we might blurt out:
　　　I was troubled by the fleeting vision of your body;
　　　in those very moments that could change our life,
　　　　　　　　we want to hide, in order to survive;
　　　　　　　　　　in order to avoid
　　　　　　　　　　being eaten by birds,
　　　　　we wish ourselves carpet, wallpaper, doors,
　　　　　instead of the great scandal that our words

might cause.)

It is perhaps that vision and those regrets that force
Tatiana to pace up and down in her room tonight.
She's trying to exhaust herself so she can sleep.
For days now she's stayed awake till dawn.
All this love and tiredness make her want to puke.
She tries to count her steps, but the hope's forlorn:
she has no self-discipline at all.

A hundred steps a hundred and one a garrison of
steps she is an army just her alone she's the military
march of her beating heart she's the general at its head
it is she who decides she won't let her emotions walk
all over her she wants order in her organs calm in her
cardiac rhythm she wants to sleep perchance to NO no
dreams she is in charge here not her ventricles not the
tentacles of her octopus bed she needs to sleep her
mind a blank no images of pencil shadings NO
steep dark line of hairs going down to NO please
just sleep just sleep let her sleep please sleeeeeep

But trying *not* to think about something
        is a battle lost in advance; your brain

will just keep asking you –

what was that thing again?

Now Tatiana's feet

are aching and her head

is still filled with pictures of Eugene.

And she still hasn't fallen asleep.

Yet another sunrise to be seen

from her window. She's high

on exhaustion and suddenly feels

invincible.

The truth is, she thinks,

I missed my chance, earlier today;

I could have   I should have   told him.

And yet . . .

And yet . . . why not!

Here, now, she will do it, she will be

the person she wants to be: someone better.

I am going, she tells herself, *to write him a letter.*

A letter of unspeakable beauty. A letter

that is honest, true, real;

lines written straight from her heart

like the straight dark line of hairs that NO NO

DON'T THINK ABOUT THAT.   I said NO.

So . . .

write this letter now, Tatiana, in haste,
instead of imagining the path of that dark line

below his waist.

Tatiana runs to her desk and picks up a pen.
Intelligent, she thinks, *be intelligent.*
She thinks she'll write something full of references.
Something spiritual. Subtle. Something to impress Eugene,
who loves quotations more than he loves his parents.
Yes, that's it!
She'll compose a letter littered with quotations.
He can have fun spotting each one
and at the same time
admire her sophistication,
while simultaneously guessing
at her feelings.
Tatiana makes several failed attempts,
which we won't list in detail right now;
it will be the task of future archivists
to decrypt those crumpled scripts.

The last one, written around three in the morning,
reads as follows:

Dear Eugene,

I shall be telling this with a sigh somewhere ages hence:
How I saw a proud rider on a horse's proud back;
Oh, how his broad clear brow in sunlight glowed!
And from underneath his helmet flowed
His coal-black curls, his flashing eyes,
For he had fed on honey-dew, and drunk the milk of Paradise.
My love, had we but world enough and time . . .
Alas! At my back I always hear Time's chariot arrive!
And as love is life, and life hath immortality,
Let me wake forever in this sweet unrest,
And so live eternally – or else swoon to death.

Tatiana contemplates her shanty-town verse,
cobbled together from others' words.
        In itself, it has to be said,
                        the poem is not
                                especially good.
        Put it this way: if Eugene does not spot
the references, he might well wonder
        what exactly she's been sniffing.
        And as the original verses were not all in the same
meter,

80

she had to plug the gaps with words of her own:

an *oh* here, a *how* there,

an *alas* where it does not belong,

and to make it rhyme,

she had to alter some of the lines,

and you can tell, a little bit, she thinks.

(Who is she kidding? It stinks!)

But the biggest problem is that none of the thoughts

are really hers.

It is the work

of a thousand others,   and yet of no one.

It is half past three in the morning when she scrunches up

the sheet of paper.

She sits down at her desk again,

concentrates and   at last   frees herself.

Sometimes, she realises, you can try too hard

to be perfect. Reaching for rhymes and rhythm when you

could write freely. Being clever when you could be sincere.

Writing a letter with ink and quill, when you could just

Open a New Message.

Eugene's email address will come in handy, after all.

Tatiana turns on her computer,

which takes ten minutes to sputter into life   (it's 2006),

and she opens her Hotmail inbox

and finds she has an email from Myspace
reminding her it's her birthday

><small>(it's not: she gave the website
>a false date of birth;
>her actual birthday is in two weeks' time)</small>

and another one, some spam, that yells

TATIANA1992

SEND A VIRTUAL CARD

TO THE PERSON YOU LOVE!!!

MORE THAN 250 ANIMATED CARDS!!!

FOR FRIENDSHIP, LOVE, CONDOLENCES

Tatiana smiles at this coincidence (which is nothing of the
kind, since she gets messages like this almost every day).

>In a corner of the screen, MSN
>lights up too.

Sometimes the little men are blue, other times grey or green;

>Eugene
>>is a little grey man.

>At this hour of the night, of course, everyone

is a little grey man.

>(Except for SmarterChild, the robot from MSN,

every insomniac's friend,
always available for weird conversations.
I used to chat with him sometimes,
because I liked the odd sensation
of conducting a discussion
with someone who couldn't answer
any important question;
just like all of us,
but at least he admitted it
instead of trying to bluff.

Have you ever fallen in love, SmarterChild?
Robots do not fall in love.
What should I write in a love letter, SmarterChild?
If I were to write a letter,
the first thing I would consider
is the person to whom I am writing.
I can't sleep, SmarterChild.

I am sorry to learn
that you are having difficulty
falling asleep.
What is the meaning of life, SmarterChild?
I am afraid that I have not been
programmed to respond to this question.

I miss SmarterChild; it's a pity
he no longer exists. Siri tries too hard to be witty.
Even though he sometimes made no sense,
I preferred SmarterChild and his wise innocence.)

Tatiana is not done with robotic questions.
She clicks on Microsoft Word,
starts to write . . .

Dear Eugene
        and right away
        it looks as though you're writing a letter
exclaims the animated paperclip, with his bulging eyes
and vicious smile
                can I help you?
        No, thanks – I'm fine.

Tatiana clicks on the X in the top right corner of the screen
and the paperclip vanishes. Now she can proceed.

She writes her message to Eugene with disconcerting ease.
No verbal acrobatics.
It is simply a message that tells him   how she feels.

It's beautiful, in its way. I kept it.   Would you like to see?

Tatiana's message
to Eugene

Good evening Eugene,

      or rather, good morning.

It was really nice to see you again today.

Recently, maybe because of the way

I'm feeling (bored), or the hot summer weather,

or maybe some other reason,

      whatever,

         sometimes I just wait

           for you to arrive.

Then I hear the creak of the garden gate,

      and there you are,

        with Lensky by your side.

But until you turn up, I'm all distracted.

I find it hard to concentrate.

    I wait and wait,

but when we're waiting, we don't really live;

reality seems unreal.

For weeks now, it's like reality's been passing me by;

        I can't touch it, I can't feel

anything

until the gate swings open and you enter our garden.

It's strange, but

only when you're there with me

do I feel like I'm where I'm supposed to be.

>The rest of the time, I'm like a girl at the window

>>watching myself live,

>>out there, down below,

>with the feeling that life is happening to

someone else

>>and I am trapped behind glass.

I know what I'm writing is not very elegant –

I don't think of myself as poetic –

>and I also know that it's probably because

I'm a bit too romantic,

>but

>>I just wanted to ask if maybe

>>>you might have feelings for me?

I do

>for you

>>by the way.

>>I've known it ever since we first met.

You've probably got loads of girls after you, though; in fact,

>I'm

sure you have to brush them off your trouser legs
all the time.

> Maybe you have a girlfriend back at home,
> that you've never mentioned?
> Maybe you don't have any feelings for me,
> after all.

Or maybe you're gay?

> Not that I have a problem

with that – no way!
But if you're not

> gay, I mean

and you don't

> have a girlfriend

and you do

> have feelings for me

then maybe

> we

> could go to see

> a movie

together, or something, one of these days.
I heard *Spider-Man*

> is out at the moment. But it doesn't have to be
> that film in particular. Anything will do.
> I like pretty much everything, honestly.

Or we could just go for a walk in the park,
or lie on the grass and gaze up at the stars (haha).
I hope I don't sound hysterical
and I hope this isn't embarrassing,

       and I really hope you don't feel like I'm pressuring
       you into anything. If you don't reply, I promise you,
I won't be upset.

        So good morning, and I'll see you soon,
        hopefully this afternoon! Better go ...
        Tatiana xoxo

The message makes a sound
like a rocket blasting off into the sky.
Tatiana imagines Eugene opening it. She imagines
      his (blue) eyes
reading it,
      line after line,
      and welling
      with tears
      of tenderness,
      perhaps.

It is four fifty-four in the morning;
      a shard of sunlight spears the plum sky.

This is exactly the letter that she'd felt deep inside.

       Tender, honest, direct.

       Sweet, yet discreet.

I know, I know.

       You couldn't hope for a better

       love letter,

       nor a worse one.

If Tatiana were to read that ten years later ... oh my God!

       That *get-me-out-of-here* moment,

       thinking: I wish I were dead,

       thinking: that wasn't me,

       it can't have been!

She would never recognise herself in those words;

she would see only the clumsy mistakes

of another girl,

someone who no longer exists:

       a shrinking violet,

       a frightened virgin,

             not someone who is studying the

             liquid elements in Caillebotte's work,

             someone who is calm when shooing

             away her supervisor's wooing.

We are hard on ourselves when we recollect the past;

we hate ourselves, in retrospect.
But I swear that at this very moment,
the moment when the message blasts off into the ether,
Tatiana feels better than she's ever felt before; not just
liberated, not just unburdened,

> but something much deeper:
> she feels *translated*, if you will;
> she feels *immortalised*.

> There now exists, outside herself, a copy of
her soul. She is proud to have brought it to life.

> Naturally, ten years later,
> this description will no longer fit.
> But the same is true of any photograph, isn't it?
> Why do we feel the need to recognise our thoughts
> ten years later, when one look in the mirror
> will show us how much we've changed?
> We put our ideas on a higher plane
> than our appearance; we tell ourselves
> that they will never change,
> our titanium thoughts, our platinum promises.
> Yes, Tatiana's words were true once,
> and time will prove them false;
> where the present caresses, now,

the past will later pinch. So what?
Tonight, those thoughts of hers are the living truth.
And, for a thought,
to be true once,
even for just one night,
is already quite a feat.

*****

The next day, or rather the same day,
Tatiana wakes at ten;
a strangely late hour for this early bird.
With her head on the pillow,
she listens, through the open window,
to the bees tapping the wisteria's purple lips.
She hears Olga sneeze (hay fever)
down in the garden.
Olga is eating her breakfast outside – Tatiana hears
the scrape of a knife buttering toast;
she hears the music from the MP3 placed in a
glass to amplify its sound.
Without looking, she knows that her sister is sitting
between the cafetiere and the butter dish
at the rusty table,   as she always does.

The song

is by Muse, a cover version, soaring and ethereal,

of 'Feeling Good'.

Olga sings along as she listens to it:

Freedom is mine,

You know how I feel

If she's singing,

that must mean that Lensky

has sent her a poem this morning.

It's a new dawn, it's a new day,

it's a new life

Tatiana gets up and goes to the window, waves to her sister

and helps her finish the song:

for me

and I'm feeling good

'It's so wonderful to hear you two sing!'

exclaims their mother.

Da-dum

Da-dum

Da-dum

Da-da-da-da-dum

It's Saturday. She's in the garden too, reading

Courrier International.

'I used to sing all the time, when I was your age.'

Tatiana hurtles downstairs to join them,
to scrape butter across toast
        and get drunk on black coffee
            in the garden already invaded from the east
by sunlight.
She and Olga talk with their eyes: both girls
are in a very good mood this morning.
        They are filled with love.
They dance and whirl,
and their mother quickly hoards this happiness while it lasts.
She knows that at fourteen or seventeen,
everything changes fast.

        From beneath her copy of *Grazia*, Olga
watches her sister spread plum jam on her bread.

        Tatiana's grown up this summer, she thinks;
she'll be fifteen in a couple of weeks,
        and there's something luminous about her now.
Olga has never thought her sister beautiful, but she cannot
deny that there's something about her that might drive
        a professor, a doctor, a solicitor wild . . .
        the kind of man who's attracted
        to the harsh rind you find
        covering any very intelligent girl.
Yes, she's sure, somewhere there must be

a guy who'll find Tatiana sexy.

Satisfied with this conclusion, Olga returns to her magazine.

HOW

TO CHOOSE THE

BEST MOISTURISER

One day this too will be of interest to her sister.

Once she is done with books and daydreaming.

AND DON'T FORGET TO REAPPLY IN THE EVENING

Tatiana, meanwhile, watches a butterfly of butter
bloom through the black liquid as she dunks toast
in her coffee.

She'll check her emails later. There's no rush.

Without meaning to, she's enjoying her youth.

*****

In the meantime, Eugene has received the message.

He's read it twice   or three times   or even
I don't know how many times exactly, but the point is,

he cares.

Yes, this message matters to him. Speaks to him.

Maybe it even touches him. Maybe.

It's hard to say. At first, he thought:

Typical.   Classic.   Normal.

Just another girl, charmed by yours truly.

Completely predictable, utterly unoriginal.

This shit happens to me every month, practically.

He was expecting it, of course. He has to admit

that he's a little bit,

I don't know, disappointed,

that she should make her feelings known,

but, at the same time, that email she wrote,

it was nicely phrased; he's flattered,

despite himself,

and kind of confused too,

and confused that he's confused.

It crosses his mind to take advantage of the

situation; become the kind of person who goes to see

Spider-Man purely so he can snare Tatiana in his web and

snog her.

But then Eugene feels uneasy,

stopped in his tracks by a pang of morality –

some kind of Catholic guilt from far away:

the thought of seducing her leaves him queasy.

He tells himself: 'She's just a kid.'

Kid is a useful term. Kid means cute.
Kid equals child, sister, daughter.
Kids are flat-chested, slender-hipped,
without soft, enticing curves.
Kid means fresh and innocent, free
of the burning desires of riper girls.
Kid equals smooth, simple and sleek;
no dangerous slopes or hidden creeks.
You tuck a kid in. You read her books,
stories to teach her about life and help her sleep.
With a kid, your duty is to educate.

Eugene feels as though he's been assigned an important task.
He knows now how he'll reply; in his head, he composes an
answer heavy with the weight

of the three years longer than Tatiana
that he's lived;
of the dozens of books more than Tatiana
that he's read;
of the numberless loves more than Tatiana
that he's had.

And here, I must interrupt the story briefly to confess
that I am not exactly sure

of the precise number of lovers Eugene's had.

He would say *a lot*.

But men often brag like that.

There's not much trace of them in the records.

And besides, he's only seventeen, so I doubt he's bedded

a hundred girls in France, a thousand and three in Spain.

But all the same,

if Eugene's already bored

of such conquests, you can bet

he must have quite a hoard.

The answer he's cooking up for Tatiana is a lesson

drawn from all those loves,

of which Tatiana's is, in his mind,

an infinitesimally small representation,

a drop in the ocean,

a typical crush, one of thousands;

he will teach her a lesson based on hard facts.

And one day

(he thinks)

she will thank him for it.

*****

And yet the hours pass

and the garden gate does not creak.

Tatiana has bitten down most of her nails. She's refreshed her Hotmail inbox thirty times and counting.
Impossible to concentrate on the Elizabeth Gaskell she's reading.

The slightest sound – the buzz of a bumblebee, the honk of a car horn, a screeching magpie, a backfiring motorbike – and she lifts up her head, suddenly on edge.

But the gate does not budge.

In this universe of strange noises, Olga
is contentedly reading *Eat Pray Love*.
Apparently, all is normal, for her.
Flexing her toes, she slaps her flip-flops against her feet.
Time passes, and Tatiana hopes that Olga
will suddenly spring up, weary of all this heat,
and wonder, at last,
what the hell her boyfriend's doing.
Her boyfriend, usually, is all she talks about,
twenty-four hours a day.
So why, today,
is she acting as if he never
existed in the first place?
As if their lives had not been changed forever
by him leading Eugene

through that garden gate?
After the fifteenth flip-flop flap, Tatiana cracks:
'Isn't Lensky coming today?' she asks,
                                    cactus-throated.
Olga, without looking up: 'No,
he's gone to visit his cousin Anne-Marie
with Eugene.'
This cousin immediately appears
                in Tatiana's overloaded mind
        as a cross between Liv Tyler and Angelina Jolie,
a Nobel-Prize-winning Olympic athlete, founder of a
fashionable charity for the benefit of humankind.
            No email that afternoon. Nor that evening.
            A night of silent screaming.

            Same time, next afternoon:
            'Isn't Lensky coming today?'
            'Yeah, he is. He told me he'd be here soon,'
            says Olga,
            instinctively glancing at her Nokia flip-phone.
            And it's true: Lensky does arrive   alone.

Tatiana can't ask any more questions; she feels as though
she's living inside a body that's no longer her own;

and bloody Olga's incurious as a stone!

Eugene's absence just sits there,

like an elephant in a deckchair.

What can she do, Tatiana,

but drink tea with this enormous absence?

Later, when Lensky's leaving,

she manages to articulate:

'So Eugene's not coming today?'

Lensky: 'Nah, he didn't feel like it.'

He didn't feel like it.

Does that mean:

1. that he's ill – he's got stomach ache, he's throwing up everywhere; or
2. that he doesn't want to see me because he feels insulted by what I wrote; or
3. that he's busy screwing Lensky's cousin (who has, since yesterday, also become a neurosurgeon); or
4. that he's afraid he won't be able to stop himself furiously kissing me?

With the exception of the first (not fantastically interesting) possibility, these scenarios will circle Tatiana's head all night.

    2:34 am.

    Still   no   email.

                        Refresh the page.

The next afternoon, Lensky
turns up at the usual time,
        escorted by Eugene's elephantine
absence,
        which, having gained twenty pounds
overnight, proceeds to break three wicker chairs, crush the
parasol and smash all the porcelain
before slumping across the forged-iron table.

    'Isn't Eugene coming?'

    'Eugene? Ah, no, he's gone to Paris to see his
parents. He'll be back tomorrow.'

    Tomorrow,

                    still nothing.
Eugene's absence is getting to know the garden well now.
It nibbles the mint leaves, terrifies the birds.

        It's absolutely absurd, Eugene's absence.
Tatiana's store of questions is all used up. One more 'Isn't
Eugene coming?' and even Lensky will fathom that she's

not asking out of politeness but passion.

After the next day, and the day after
that, and finally the day after *that*, Tatiana's superhuman
hopefulness runs dry,

and she starts to await
the daily creak of the gate
that greets

the absence
of Eugene.
To her surprise, she gets used to this routine

non-event.
It's as if she's closed the brackets around Eugene.
From moment to moment, she is certain/not certain

that he existed/did not exist in her life.
This doubt seems unimportant. She loves him still,

of course,

but Tatiana's love has never depended
on anything particularly real;
even when she's not quite sure the thing she loves exists,

it doesn't alter the way that she feels.

In moments of lucidity, she is fully aware that it's
because of her that he's disappeared.

And so, feeling responsible for his absence,
she takes great care to make it welcome here;

she holds its hand
and whispers secrets in its ear.

*****

One day   a thousand years later,
          or maybe it was just a week,
                    the gate creaks open, and suddenly,
                    here's Lensky
                    and   'Eugene!'
                              (cries Olga)
'We missed you!   Where have you been?'

                              Eugene is there, in the flesh.
                    He has taken the place of his absence.
Tatiana was completely unprepared for this event.
She had poured the non-cup of tea and taken out
the non-tin of biscuits for her fat phantom friend.
She was not expecting to feel so shocked
if Eugene ever did come back.
Her heart takes the lift
                    up to her larynx,
                    where it gets stuck
                    hammering against the walls of her

neck.

Faced with something utterly unforeseen,

    animal instinct:

fight   *or*   *flight.*

Tatiana, faced with the real Eugene,

       goes for the one on the right.

    Suddenly she has something more important to
do upstairs. What? Who cares! Revisions, reading, ironing,
watching *Who Wants to Be a Millionaire?* ...

    Entering the garden, Eugene finds only the
absence of Tatiana; and it has to be said that it stings him,

      that absence,

like a fresh little graze on the skin of the world.

    Through the window, Tatiana hears him say:

    'Isn't Tatiana here?'

    'Oh yeah, she is, I just saw her run upstairs,'

    replies Olga.

So now he knows: she fled. She's a coward and a fool.

Tatiana takes refuge in the bathroom,

    the only believable excuse that she can find

for having run upstairs just as he arrived.

    But now she's in a bind because, as soon as they
hear the toilet flush,

everyone will expect her back outside.

For a moment she wavers on the landing floor
like one of those spinning tops
that, for a few instants of perfect grace,
express their disagreement
with gravity,
refuse to
topple

. . .

when suddenly
in front of her, Eugene appears.
Thirty times bigger than he was before,
a backlit ghost surging up from a crack in the floor.
Tatiana cannot speak.
Eugene seems to hesitate, just for a moment, and
then,

he tells her . . .

*****

but perhaps it is not yet time
for us to know

what he tells her.
After all, Eugene, ten years later,
can hardly recall what he said,
        and it wouldn't be right to remind him here and now.
That would be too easy, all in all.
And anyway, all of this is connected
to another tragic incident,
which also weighs in the balance,
and which I will tell you about at a more strategic moment.

                                So, on that cliffhanger,
                                let's fast-forward in time
                                to ten years later.

        We'd left Tatiana in the library, Eugene on his way
                to his grandfather's grave, each of them
                slightly disorientated, a little tense,
                        still in suspense
                    after seeing each other again;
                but, for now, of those two tensions,
                it's Eugene's that requires our attention.

3

The first thing Eugene did when he arrived at the cemetery
was to look for his mother,
his father, his sisters, his grandmother,
so he could avoid them at all costs.
At that moment, his one overriding desire,
before going to pay his tributes to the deceased,
was to search for Tatiana –
or google her, at least.
Why had he never thought to do this before?
All those wasted years!
He could have googled her a million times or more
from the comfort of his own home.
He could have set daily alerts!
Then he'd have been prepared,
instead of standing here, fingers shaking,
brain ready to burst,

begging the sky for urgent information
and cursing the crapness of the 4G reception

    in the cemetery.

    He'd already spotted his family, all in black –

    umbrella uncles, cockroach cousins,

    and the old man in the coffin –

but the page was taking an eternity to load; all he saw
was one line at the top: '219,000 results'.
He seriously doubted
that he could read through 219,000 results
before his absence at the funeral was spotted.

    Hiding out one aisle over from the hole

    that awaited his dead kin,

    behind a tawdry gypsum gravestone

    engraved with Tremblay

    (a name that matched the state that he was in),

    Eugene shook his phone, an electronic superstition,

    a little like his grandfather,

    in the early days of television,

    would wiggle the aerial to catch the waves better.

Different devices. Same anger

    that they just don't seem to understand our desires

    instinctively.

    Still the page didn't load. *Stupid bloody technology.*

He tried to find a network manually.

'Is Eugene still not here?' asked his sister Evelyne.

'I'll call him,' replied his sister Marguerite.

Vibrations.

A little green cartoon phone –

the idiotic icon of a telephone invented by those
condescending cretins at Apple –

appeared on his screen,
blocking Tatiana's 219,000 public secrets.

Duty-bound, he answered:

'Hello?'   'Hello, Eugene?

Where are you?'   'Just arrived.'

And he emerged from behind the Tremblay tomb,
to the surprise of his relatives,

who had not come

to play hide-and-seek among the graves.

He dispensed dry hellos and curt cold kisses,
cursing inwardly, furious at the idea

that his screen was now slowly percolating
tidbits about Tatiana that only his pocket could see.

The ceremony began.

The priest, as if drawn by a child

(black triangle, white square),

recited a litany of mild

praise, and then

it was Eugene's turn.

His speech was saved on his phone, of course.

He took it out – quick squint –

and there it was, a glimpse

of the first page of results: the name of the website,

keywords in bold – 'Tatiana', 'Reinal' – and each

description,

three lines long

cut suddenly

short.

sorbonne.fr With a bachelor's degree

and a Master in History of Art, **Tatiana Reinal**

has since 2012 been composing her PhD thesis

under the supervision of Professor Leprince. Her

analysis is centred on ... <Click to open>

caillebotteonline.fr ... must hope that

the upsurge of interest in Gustave Caillebotte

over the past thirty years is indicative of an

enduring revival.' Text by **Tatiana Reinal**. Share

<Click to open>

inlovewithlabelleepoque.fr . . . contact **Tatiana Reinal** (vice-president) for details concerning themed walks in Paris . . . <Click to open>

international-society-for-art-history.com . . . cannot sever the economics of impressionism from its aesthetics, as **Tatiana Reinal** underlines . . . <Click to open>

marmiton.fr **tatiana_reinal** Thank you for this recipe. I replaced cognac with grand marnier and it worked very well. Even better warmed up . . . <Click to open>

'He's speechless with emotion,'
whispered his sister Evelyne,
and Eugene had the alarming realisation
that everyone was waiting for him to speak,
while all he wanted to know
        was what recipe Tatiana had liked.
Frustrated and panicking, he hid the window
        showing the results, and looked for his notes.
        Finding them, he stammered out

a speech that lacked
his usual eloquence,
which everyone interpreted as evidence
of his deep sincerity.
As soon as the speech was over,
between the tearful thank yous of family friends
and two kisses from his mother in a cloud of perfume,
he restarted Chrome,
and his phone

went black.

The battery was dead.
For a moment, he thought about
throwing himself headlong into the hole
intended for his grandfather,
and then his mind filled with other thoughts
and he saw
the cemetery speeding around him,
quicker and quicker:

and what if   she was googling him too?
searching for him on Facebook and Twitter?
Eugene's results were not great, he knew:

- His professional page on the website of the
  consultancy firm where he was Chief Business
  Adviser for France / Eastern Europe / Russia.

- His LinkedIn page listing a Modern Languages degree
  + a masters from a mediocre college in America.
- A page of client recommendations: *The Slavs can
  be crafty: if you have any business dealings or
  negotiations with them, Eugene will help you.*

And somewhere in the depths of cyberspace,
an Excel document listing the results for a go-kart race
in La Rochelle, in which he finished seventh.
The Google results of a Nowhere Man,
someone whose very soul was grey,
someone so deeply *nothing* that between
seventeen and twenty-seven,
all that was listed
was the simple fact that he had carried on breathing,
kept on existing,

                              that he'd aged a bit,
that he'd let the current of life carry him towards the sea
            of further education, a job, a small apartment:
            middle-class Parisian mediocrity.
The Eugene who'd hatched from the Eugene of before,
            brutally exposed by the Internet,
            would not impress Tatiana one bit,
            only make her

yawn endlessly, perhaps even rejoice
at the choice
that he himself – *oh God!* –
had made to reject her.
A bullet dodged is what she'd say
to herself, thanking her lucky stars that he
dismissed her so unceremoniously.
She'd say to herself: you might have wasted
ten years of your life with a man who did nothing better
than become a Chief Business Adviser.

Yes.   But then
                                                                              again,
maybe, if he . . .

I mean, if things hadn't gone that way,
he might be a very different man today.
He might have lived a truly exciting life
    with her, crossing oceans and continents,
      reading Kerouac and Kundera in tacky motels,
        eating chicken feet in China, dancing all night,
          trekking through the Amazonian rainforest . . .
Jesus Christ! How boring his life was in reality!
She was bound to see how dull he was, this Eugene, the
very worst

of him starkly revealed by Google.

And the worst of it was: it was all completely factual.

       'He looks devastated,' observed his sister Agnes.

       'Just completely devastated by Grandad's death.'

Eugene, however, was wrong to fret;

Tatiana had googled him half a dozen times

over the past ten years, I'll bet;

       in idle moments, increasingly rare,

       while distracted by daydreams,

       or just feeling bored,

she'd let her fingertips stroll across the keyboard

and pick out the letters of his name, each little square

       making her feel

like a pianist playing an almost forgotten song,

       a sort of wonder at finding it again,

that name   that she had so often sighed,

       dissected and reassembled in her head,

that name   that, like any teenage girl,

she had scrawled all over the pages of her journal,

       engraved into her plastic protractor.

     And even at eighteen, even after,

into her twenties, each time Tatiana typed out the letters

      E – U – G – E – N – E,

her mind was filled
with the same music as previously,
and her fingertips tripped
over each thrilling letter:
three tender, trilling *E*s,
pushing apart
the three detonations at the heart
of Eugene's name:
the *G*, the *U*, the *N*.

And as for the results she found
when she googled him,
she didn't mind; it was the melody of *you-jean*
that made her heart pound.

That evening, when Eugene was at last alone,
he went through the list of results – not all
219,000, of course, only the first page or two,
the others being red herrings
(including a large number of specialists in porn,
who chose Tatiana as their *nom d'amour*
and wore very dangly earrings).
And he sorted through the pieces
of the Tatiana puzzle, which included:
• A scholarly core, filled with dazzling successes.

A baccalauréat at seventeen; finished first in her Literature class; won a prize in Philosophy; several articles published; made speeches at international conferences . . .

• A few eclectic pastimes around the edges.

Gave themed walks in Paris for tourists who loved books. A part-time painter too, with some pretty works: not especially original, but nicely done. She had her own blog – not many visitors, and not often updated, but fun – where she chronicled the films she'd seen, the exhibitions she'd visited, the books she'd read.

Her latest favourite was *HHhH* by Laurent Binet.

She described it as 'daring, inspired and funny'.

(Eugene decided that he hated Laurent Binet.)

• Between the centre and the edges, nothing:

a gaping hole.

Social life? *Nothing.*

Love life? *Nada.*

Sex life? *Zilch*!

Eugene tried to think rationally:

it was pretty normal

not to find online any specific details

of her intimate relations. What was he hoping for?

'I HAVE NOTHING AGAINST SODOMY, declares

Tatiana Reinal. <Click to open>'?

That was not a realistic expectation.
But all the same, she might have had a Facebook page,
offering a little bit of information.

Eugene hated Facebook,
and obviously wasn't on it himself.
But he found it pretty outrageous
that Tatiana wasn't either. How dare she.
The loves of her life, if she'd had any,
if she had any now,
had left no trace.

Eugene paused on a result: the announcement of a
speech to be given by Tatiana
(the real one, not a porn star),
open to the general public,
the following week (Saturday),
as part of a festival at the Musée d'Orsay,
with the title:
'The young man at the window: what is he looking at?'
Eugene did not really care about
the object of the young man's gaze,
but this would be his chance
to see Tatiana again,
without having to call her. He could pretend
to be visiting the museum, just to get some

culture, and then ...

                                    Tatiana, hey!
What an amazing coincidence, seeing you today
for the second time in a week,

                        after ten years of nothing at all!
            Play it cool:
since we're both here, why not go for a bite?

        Of food, I mean.   I don't mind if we stay out late,
                I've got nothing planned tonight.
                Which is uncharacteristic, I should point out,
                cause normally on Saturday,
                I go out with friends.
                I have friends, lots of them,   but they're away,
                so anyway – what do you think?   Fancy a drink?

But
Eugene had to admit
that there was a possibility
she wouldn't believe his tale of chance,
the idea that he was there by sheer coincidence.
So why not just confess he wanted to see her?

                And why 'confess', in fact?
                Just tell her, with honesty,
                intelligence, tact,
                the way she told him once how she felt ...

                                            119

What exactly was it that she had said?

He only had the vaguest recollection,

It was pretty mind-boggling, thinking about it now:

how could Eugene, the undisputed king

of remembering a thousand

useless facts and names and dates,

enabling him to crush his opponents at Trivial Pursuit,

prompting all his friends to say he should be on TV

because he'd be bound to win *Mastermind* or *Jeopardy!* ...

how could someone with such a brilliant mind

suddenly find

such a hole in his memory?

How was he able to recall

the capital of Nepal, every island in the Pacific Rim,

but not that crucial thing:

the words of a young girl who loved him?

He remembered that the letter had been

beautiful;

that went without saying,

since the girl who wrote it had grown up to be

the Tatiana of today.

Of course her words had been deep and true

If only he'd known what to do

with them. If only he'd kept a copy of that letter ...

he could use it for inspiration now

        or, even better,

make subtle reference to the things she had felt for him,

    as a way of expressing what he felt for her.

    Frantically he searched through his inbox:

did he still have it, the email that she'd sent?   No.

He'd changed his account to gmail after that.

Tatiana's words were not the only things he'd forgotten.

That summer didn't linger.

The place where the garden ought to be

      was a desert

      in his memory.

           Almost nothing remained,

not the good things, nor the bad,

not her love, nor their pain.

He couldn't even find a single message from Lensky,

not one confirmation that they'd ever been friends.

Even the few photos of the two of them he used to keep

were lost when his hard drive died.

    This was before Dropbox.

    2006: a lost world,

    trapped on the other side

    of a technological divide.

He knew there was no point googling Lensky,
of course.

The results would not have changed in the past decade:
a small piece in *Le Figaro*,
with a few biographical details
and a photograph of Lensky smiling,
the caption reading:
his name, open brackets, date of birth
then a dash
and another date, seventeen and a half
years later, close brackets.
And that's all.

*****

At the library that day, Tatiana
did not spend a huge amount of time

thinking   about Eugene.
Just a little bit, now and then, as you'd expect.
With less intensity,

with far less urgent necessity
than ten years before. Of course, she'd been shocked
to see him again,

but she had notes to take, she had Caillebotte to consider,
          she had to write a summary
          of that book by Valéry
          (no simple feat) ...
     there were a thousand obligations in her life these days:
the paper for next Thursday's symposium to reread;
preparing for that presentation she had to deliver
          at the Musée d'Orsay
          next Saturday;
coffee with a friend (who was taking her dissertation viva)
at four
     and a whole list of other responsibilities, other tasks ...
     Admin. A thing she kept postponing:
     preparing for her flight to San Francisco
     (she was going there soon for a research trip,
     with the possibility, if Leprince was to be trusted,
          of a permanent
          academic position on offer, but ...
     later – she'd think of it later). For now:
     flight-booking, bag-packing, list-checking,
     book-buying – *The Rough Guide to San Francisco*? –
     to help her find places to go
     sightseeing, bar-hopping, window-shopping ...
     Yet she didn't exactly know

why, but today Tatiana felt like putting it off.
She'd do all that later. Focus on other stuff,
like finding gifts on Etsy for her nieces' birthday,
(Olga had twins; they'd turned two yesterday),
and booking train tickets online, the system crashed
all the bloody time
(she was going to her cousin's wedding
in May,
at a chateau near Montpellier);
she also had to confirm her Airbnb reservation
(a horses' stable until its recent renovation!)
and then after she left the library, she had to, um, let me see
that shopping list . . . oh yes, buy cat litter (clumping) for the,
um, cat . . . obviously,
and muesli
(without raisins)
toothpaste (sensitive gums)
La Laitière yoghurts (vanilla/plum)
+ don't forget (underlined three times)
Cillit Bang (for the bathroom tiles)!
And when she got home, she had to check her bank account
online.

Home, for Tatiana, was a little studio flat in
Boulogne Billancourt; 750 euros per month in rent.

Sasha the cat had access to the roof through a vent.

Tatiana's life was no longer
what it had been when she was younger:
                    a blank canvas, drum-tight,
to be decorated with needle, scissors, thread,
gilt-embroidered with a thousand daydreams,
colours bright . . .
No. Now it was the life of someone new: a busy,
                                        devoted,
                                        studious young woman,
                                        a serious scholar,

                someone
who had lists of things to tick off on Google Calendar,
and who also had to deal with unexpected problems
                                        such as this one:

                                        Dear Tatiana,

            In order to celebrate the imminent publication
                Of your magnificent article on Degas,
        I would like to present you with this humble invitation
            To meet me at Angelina's at four for hot chocolate
            And delicious macarons the day after tomorrow.

Please say yes, or I'll be plunged into sorrow!

G. Leprince.

It was perhaps not surprising,
amid the gravity-defying
act of juggling
that constituted Tatiana's life forever more,
that the place allotted to Eugene should appear
considerably smaller than before.

And yet,

and yet,
somewhere in her head, perhaps in her inner ear,
a tiny sound could be heard, revealing
the intermittent presence of Eugene,
like a little jolt, repeating,
beating,
against the inside of her chest at times, a tension
felt in those rare moments   of inattention
as she turned a page   *Eugene*
or underlined a phrase   *Eugene*
As she wrote a boring email,

Eugene hissed like static
between the lines . . .

Dear Sir   I am writing to you about

   Eugene   *Eugene*

the possibility of seeing   the sketch made by

     Eugene   *Eugene*

Caillebotte during the summer he spent with

          Eugene

          (etc.)

And so it was with Eugene pulsing in her mind,

   images of their reunion still flickering in her brain,

that Tatiana took the metro home,

and then the suburban train.

She had lots of things to do before going to bed,

but chose instead,

   for once,

  to go to sleep early,

  with Sasha a shapka on her head.

  She checked that she didn't have any new emails,

  just in case,

not that she was expecting any but   anyway,

          no,

no new emails from him.

Nor any texts.
He must have asked for her number just out of politeness.

Telephone in hand, head warmed by the cat,
she spent a long time
observing the contours of her studio flat,
dimly lit by a single lamp
that crayoned the Ikea furniture in grey.
She didn't dream of anything special,
but the next day,
woken by her alarm,
she noticed that the phone was still in bed with her,
nestled under her arm.

*****

That week, Eugene felt   excited.
He was filled with energy.
He was filled with enthusiasm.
He felt pretty glorious, all in all,
as excited as a kid on Christmas Eve,
waiting for Santa to call.
He found it really really hard
to be patient,   to wait

for the following Saturday,   for their 'date'.
Eugene who, as an adolescent,
had had a relationship with time
            that we might characterise as jaded,
            indifferent, passive, bored,
            who, as a teenager, had never impatiently
            waited for anything –
            seriously, nothing at all –
      had become, as an adult, like everyone else.
(You can give his phone the credit – or the blame –
for that particular development.)   Like everyone else,
he waited vaguely for the next thing, always the same:
the next email, the next weather forecast,
the next election, the next plane crash,
the next death of a singer from the 1980s,
the next terrorist attack, the next pay cheque;
an adult with a miniature attention span,
like everyone else, refreshing, updating,
nibbling at time like a ham baguette.
            All the same, the way this adult Eugene waited
            was not – in normal circumstances – impatient;
                  he rarely said *I can't wait,*
I'm looking forward to this or that, it'll be great ...
            he was never in any great hurry;

he was just a young man whose *ennui*,
which had once inhabited his entire being,
was now just
a nagging pulse in the tip of his thumb,
beating out the measure of the passing seconds
by pressing an icon on a screen.
He was used to his hope feeling numb,
used to hoping for nothing in particular;
not like this hope he felt now –
for something precious, powerful, precise.

Now, suddenly, his shapeless hope
had taken the exact outline of Tatiana.
Suddenly he was waiting for a *soon*,
a living, breathing human;
he was no longer waiting just to kill time
and his hope was no longer vague and viscous,
but vital and vivacious;
a clear hope, easily summarised in three words –
Saturday / Tatiana / Orsay
– a hope that he could build and decorate.

He dreamed of it every night and he dreamed of it every day,
of the look on her face when she'd spot him in the crowd,

of all the intelligent things that he'd say

          about Manet

          and Degas

     (he'd been memorising their Wikipedia pages),

    and how that conversation

    would reveal their ravenous mutual attraction,

    his insistent, hers impatient,

how the two of them, in their desperate desire

to be together,

would hail a taxi . . .

would zip through Paris . . .

     no, no, it'd take too long, they couldn't delay,

      so they'd make love there and then, in Orsay,

behind the big statue of the polar bear,

         or anywhere,

really, anywhere at all: the nearest toilet stall would do!

And when they were done, *then* they'd hail a cab

    and head back to the refuge of Eugene's bed

       (note to self: change the sheets)

    all night Saturday they'd stay,

    and all day Sunday too

        (buy some croissants).

And Eugene imagined the lovemaking

(prolonged and beautiful).

And Eugene imagined the pillow talk
(profound and insightful).
Because while there is no denying
       that Eugene was extremely eager to uncover
       just what Tatiana was hiding
       beneath her clothing,
      he also wanted to penetrate the whole
of her; he wanted access to her heart, her mind,
her soul;
he wanted her hands not only for caresses
but as commas in all the sentences she would speak,
      all the secrets she would share,
         he wanted her ears
not only as recipients of kisses
and whispered sweet nothings,
         but to listen
to all the things he had to tell her
about his childhood, his heart, his youth,
his visions of a future that suddenly shone bright
because of her;
         he wanted her mouth
not only to kiss him
but for the words it contained,
he wanted them to pour over him

in a rain of Tatiana-ness;

        he wanted her eyes

     not only closed in orgasm or sleep,

     but wide open, pupils dilating deep

     as she remembered, eyelids creasing with laughter,

yet another story she just needed to tell.

Because there was so much

they had to say to each other after

       all those conversations cut dead

       by that sad decade,

       and now they had to continue them,

       finish them, take them in new directions,

find themselves again lost in reflection,

      where were we again?

           oh yeah ... you go first

They'd hunger for each other's ideas

     over plates of croissants; thirst

       for each other's words

         over bowls of coffee.

Eugene wanted all of this: the wordless love in bed

and all the love and words

and wonders in Tatiana's head;

to explore the universe in a grain of sand

and taste the glory of eternity in one weekend.

To be with her –
that was all . . .
all he yearned for and all he lacked.
To be with her until the sun turned black.

And on Monday morning   *I have to go to the library now*
No, stay with me   No, really, I must   Please stay
Eugene, listen   It's important to me   I know, but
But nothing, Tatiana: stay!   Oh, okay! But only for today
But in the end, when tomorrow came,
so would she,
and the day after that, and the day after that, endlessly!
This frenzy of fantasies
was too much for Eugene's brain:
he was agitated, antsy, so eager for Saturday
that life seemed to be moving
in a slow-motion replay
and he was like the driver of a car in a traffic jam:
On his way to work   *Fuck, what's wrong with the*
metro? Why's it so slow?
as if the metro might take him direct to her door.
At the bagel store

Where's my bloody bagel, eh?
I'm not just going to wait here all bloody day!

Are you still trying to catch the smoked salmon or what?

At the supermarket   *Express line my arse!*

                                                        What a farce!

And worst of all, at work, where his impatience took on a somewhat

                    passive-aggressive tone:

          'I would appreciate it if you would kindly respond to the last email I sent.'

          'Unfortunately, I must point out that you have not yet made the required payment.'

          'It might be a good idea, re: the contract (please find attached), if you would bother signing it the way it's supposed to be signed, by initialling each page, if you don't mind.'

'Everything okay, Eugene? You seem a bit stressed today.'
(Fourth colleague to the left in the open-plan office.)

                    'Everything's fine, although it would be nice
                    if people would leave me to work in peace.'

                              At times, in fact, his tone
                              was active-aggressive, even rude,
                              although thankfully only
                              in his head, not out loud:

'Relax – you might have a heart attack!'

And you might get a knee in the nutsack
'What are you doing this weekend?'
A more beautiful girl than you've ever had
And as Eugene worked in three languages, he expressed
his impatience trilingually:

> *Can't wait can't wait*
> *J'ai tellement hâte*
> *Ia s neterpenyem zhdu*
> *Saturday Samedi Subbota*
>> *Tatiana Tatiana Tatiana*

Convention dictates
that Eugene's feelings be chaste,
the kind of thing a prince might think –
rescuing a damsel in distress or gently kissing her lips.
But I have access to secret corridors in his mind;
I have peeked through certain keyholes in certain doors
and some of the things I've seen ...
well, I'd love to tell you more,
but my editors are watching me.
So make an effort of imagination.
Picture for yourself a less censored version.

> Inside the head of our handsome hero, then,
> the scenes overlapped, crashing into each other,

with no respect for chronological order,
            as if someone had tangled up the rolls of film,
so he could watch, at the same time, different shots . . .
He saw an unmade bed in the middle of the museum,
white sheets like thick whipped cream,
and atop the bed, Tatiana,
delivering her speech on Caillebotte,
and as she smiled, he saw – where her teeth should gleam –
            the delicate lace of her lingerie,
            and Monet's *Water Lilies*
            like a watermark on her skin.
Sounds, too, intermingled: he heard her talk about
painterly technique
            and listened to the bedsprings creak.
                The result was surrealist, a rhapsody
                of rapid erotica: Luis Buñuel in a blender.
So there *was* something creative in his grey man's soul; he
wished she could have shared his thoughts in this moment.
All these years, his imagination had been dormant,
            locked in lethargy, a Sleeping Beauty waiting
            for her to kiss his lips and finally wake it.
The question gnawed at Eugene all that week:
            where was all this
            before their chance meeting? What he meant

137

by *all this* was   this vitality,

                                               heart speeding,

                                               this energy,

                                               this ascent

                                    to the higher sensations . . .

               where was it all, before she reappeared?

                         This vivacity, this elation,

               were they already inside him?

                         This purpose, this emotion,

               did he owe it all to her?

It was like when you visit the eye doctor, and he changes

your lenses:

               that little glass circle is all you need

               to bring the world into focus,

               and you exclaim inside your head

               I'd never have believed that life could be so vivid –

                         where have I been? What's this new world?

At last, Eugene felt fully aware of his existence:

he sensed the working parts, the cogs, the wheels,

the minuscule movements,

he could feel

               the private pulsing of this life inside his mind;

               this life that, before,

               had been so hazy and unformed

shone now like a cut diamond.
He felt convinced that he   and he alone   could now
                perceive this life and world as they truly were;
                that he was the only one
                to grasp its secrets.

                                I was blind and now I see,
not like all the others,
poor bastards, they're still stuck in that blur . . .

                I'm sure that you recognise this feeling.
                        Love is so astonishing,
        the way it gives sudden shape to our formless expectations,
                        intense colours to our inner landscape,
                        upgrades our life to high definition
                        and convinces us that everyone else
                                is still trapped in the cave
                                from which we have escaped.
                        Later, when we've come down
                        from this 3D IMAX romance,
        when the happiness we feel is more balanced,
                more gentle, more nuanced, less mental,
                        and we meet the eye of another,
                        someone who is obviously in love,
                their vision razor-sharp, their eyes so wide,

we know what they're thinking of us, inside:
Poor girl, her life's so grey.
And we envy them a little, even as we smile
at their arrogance
and we want to reply:
Ah, but I've seen
the same things you're seeing now,
I've seen it all and I expect
that I'll see it all again someday.
Because those love goggles that you're wearing,
those universe-altering specs,
those glasses that make you feel so daring,
I've worn them before, and I daresay
that I'll wear them again someday.

Crushed by the wait, he was tempted to write to her. He started dozens of texts and emails. But he couldn't decide on anything,
not the beginning, not the middle, not the end

Dear Tatiana
Hello Tatiana
Hi Tatiana
Hola guapa

I wanted to warn you that I'll be there on Saturday

'warn' sounds a bit threatening,

doesn't it?

I'll see you Saturday   *flat*   I will probably be able to
make it to the museum on Saturday   *impersonal*
There's a chance I may be present on Saturday

stupid phrasing

It is possible that I will come on Saturday

it's possible we'll both come on Saturday

This was, he knew, becoming an obsession.

Dear Tatiana, I've been thinking about

you a lot, since the other day   *how to*

Tatiana, I haven't really thought about

much else since the other day   *make*

Oh Tatiana, you are literally all I have thought

about since the other day   *a girl*

My darling Tatiana, I find it completely

impossible to get you out of my head *freak out*

So, in the end, he didn't write to her at all.

Besides, what would have been the point? He would be
there on Saturday – she would see that for herself.

All these hesitations
were also, in private,
connected to the uncertainty felt by Eugene
regarding the nature of Tatiana's relations
with her thesis supervisor.
He could hardly make a grand declaration
before finding out if she had a thing for that moron.
Saturday would be his chance to observe them together
(how that word *together* made him sick),
to seek out clues as to whether
their relationship was more than platonic:
those singular glances, dense with significance, that pass
between two people caught up in a romance,
particularly when it's a secret;
the way they keep touching each other on the arm or the
shoulder for no reason whatsoever,
those incomprehensible allusions,
giving rise to wry smiles
that vanish in confusion.
That week, the role played by Leprince in Eugene's
fantasies, though relatively minor, was also intriguing:
sometimes he was an antagonist, the bad guy,
catching them unaware,
behind the statue of the polar bear.

142

Furious, he threatened them.

Tatiana then told Eugene

that Leprince was guilty

of sexual harassment, so the two men fought

and Eugene won, obviously.

In other daydreams, Leprince's name came up in the
middle of a discussion

on the pillow that he shared with Tatiana:

she told him *no, we're not sleeping together;*

we tried it once, but the poor man

suffers from erectile dysfunction.

So that was how Leprince was seen

in all the scenes of Eugene's daydreams:

an old man, successively aggressive and impotent,

sexually obsessive, lonely and obscene.

It never crossed his mind that Tatiana might have her
heart set on someone else, someone younger, a student, a
childhood friend, some guy she met on Tinder.

Leprince was the enemy,

not some ordinary Lucas/

Thomas/Xavier.

It was Leprince, that loser,

that ancient, pompous poseur,

who he had to annihilate for her.

(I'm no psychologist,
and besides it's really none of my business,
but don't you have the feeling that
the evil/impotent old bore
in Eugene's fantasies might have rather
less to do with Leprince and a little more
to do with Eugene's relationship with his father?)

At last Friday night arrived. In his attic flat,
filled with demonic energy, almost a sort of rage,
Eugene cleaned and tidied, dusted and swept,
changed the sheets on the bed,
threw out all his old crap and kept
only what might impress his new love:
he reordered his books (Perec in front, Asterix behind),
put a pack of condoms in the drawer of his bedside table –
open the box or leave it shut?
open makes me look like the kind of guy who invites girls
to his pad every night – a slut –
but closed makes me look like a virgin,
either that or the guy
who bought the pack just for tonight,
what did I do the last time I brought a girl home?
(the last time was several months ago)

I don't know. I didn't care last time – that's the reality:
I couldn't have cared less what that girl thought of me.
In the end he opened it, left the twelve silver-coloured
blister packs   *twelve? is that all?*

        I should have bought more   in the drawer.
Just before midnight he messed the flat up again
because he thought it looked too neat,

                casually tossing a shirt
                over the arm of chair
                as no one ever does, anywhere,
        untidying up his desk –
        three paperclips, two pens
scattered improbably over a pile of concert tickets/bank
statements/an advert for a play,
        and finally went to bed, and finally

                it was tomorrow: Saturday,

finally, this day he'd waited for so long,
finally this bus he'd ridden a hundred times in his head,
finally this queue of tourists outside the Musée d'Orsay,
                      inexplicable
        finally this glass door,   *rhinoceros*

145

finally this polar bear,

against which they'd made love

a thousand times in his fantasies,

finally this Room 32, where she was preparing to speak . . .

finally her!

He drank her in,

noting things

haphazardly:

dark turquoise poplin dress, accentuating her hips,

black jacket, black boots, black hair tied back,

the curve of her calves matching the curve of her lips,

small watch – grey leather strap –

on her wrist

and a pair of pearl earrings, pale pink.   That's it.

Ten seconds of disappointment – *That's Tatiana? That's all?*

She'd starred

in his dreams in too many guises, too many roles,

that, in truth, it was hard,

inevitably,

not to be a little bit put out by the sight

of Tatiana shrunk by reality.

But then,

in the eleventh second . . . joy:

*Yes, that's Tatiana! That's all
Tatiana!*

Eugene felt stunned by her singular wholeness,

her only Tatiana-ness: it was her,

he recognised her,

and she was a thousand times more

than the thousand shes she'd been before.

Floored by this miracle,

he contemplated her the way

a mouse might contemplate the Milky Way.

As for Tatiana,

standing in front of her painting,

if she was surprised to see Eugene

in her field of vision

between

View of Rooftops and *Pinks and Clematis*
(Effect of Snow)   *in a Crystal Vase*
          (Caillebotte/Manet

in case you're interested)

well, she didn't let it show.

Tatiana was there
to talk about *Young Man at His Window*,
a Caillebotte canvas rarely shown in exhibition,
from the private collection of an American,
currently on loan to the museum.
The picture represented a man, from behind, observing,
through the window of a Parisian house,
an almost empty avenue,
where a young woman was walking,
dwarfed by the Haussmann-style buildings all around;
behind her, a horse pulled a carriage.
All was bathed in sugar-white sunlight.
Tatiana was there
to communicate her knowledge and love of this painting to
a motley group of people:
friends of the museum, tourists, students, and others
drawn only by curiosity;
and facing her   on the wooden floor,
sitting cross-legged, wide-eyed and chubby-cheeked,
was a handful of children.

                                                    Tatiana was not there
to focus on any one particular person in the audience,
and while, yes,
she had to confess
she was a little intrigued by Eugene's presence
            I like that Fair Isle jumper   (and beauty)
                        it shows off his shoulders
she wasn't about to let that distract her from her duty.

TATIANA   Thank you for coming, thank you, everyone,
           for coming this afternoon, are you sitting
           comfortably? not too cold on the floor?
           everyone okay?
           Good, then I'll begin.
           Who can tell me   okay, we've started
           nice easy question
           who can tell me what they see in this picture?
CHILDREN   A man!
TATIANA   A man, very good. And what is he doing,
           who can tell me what he's doing, this man?
CHILDREN   He's looking out the window!
TATIANA   He's looking out the window.   Very good.
           And what is he looking at   do you think?
CHILDREN   A horse!!!

CHILD 1   I've been horse riding at Nan's house.

CHILD 2   Me too. I rode a horth wonth.

ADULT 1   I reckon he's looking at the pretty girl!

(Laughter)

TATIANA   Maybe he's looking at the horse, maybe he's
           looking at the   lady in the street,
           we don't know   maybe what he's looking at
           is
           hidden from our view by his body,
           or maybe he's not really looking at anything
           in particular.
           Don't you just sometimes   look
           through the window   at nothing
           in particular?

CHILDREN   Yes!!! (sometimes I / but one time / shhh
           / I've got a window / my mum says /
           [inaudible] / mustn't lean out the window)

TATIANA   In your opinion,
           why is he there, this man,
           looking out the window?

ADULT 1   He's unemployed! He's on benefits. He's
           got nothing to do all day but stare out the
           window.

(Laughter)

Eugene added this man to his mental list
of people to be eliminated:
he daydreamed about shooting him in the head
right here, in this hall,
his brains spurting out in a gush of pink and red
splattering over the Pissarro on the wall.
Then he started thinking of gentler things,
lulled by the soft music
of Tatiana's voice as she continued her presentation,
punctuated by the joyful cries of the children
and interrupted occasionally by that intolerable clever dick;
he watched as she restored order, subtle and serene,
with her diagonal voice, which piped up like a flute,
slender, silver, soothing,
slicing through the philharmonic murmur of the group.
He wanted it all to himself, that soprano calm,
all for him,
that sinuous melody,
winding itself around him like a dream.

This need he felt was more than desire,
a fact from which Eugene drew a weird pride;
he imagined not only
that he held her

tight to his chest,

not only

that he undressed her

while his tongue described

the curve of her breasts,

but also – and most of all –

that she embraced him in turn,

and took him by the hand,

delicately, aware of his fragility.

(Kind of surprising,

since up to then,

fragile was not something he thought

that he could be.)

TATIANA   So,   in the nineteenth century, there was

in the literature of the time,

a particular type of person

who observed, who didn't

do anything very much

except observe the city,   does anyone know

what we call   people of that kind

yes, over there?   no, not you, professor

that's cheating, you already know the answer.

Even Leprince and his pompous pontifications –

'Flaneur' was the term in vogue for such people, it's said

– and Tatiana's teasing replies

Yes, a flaneur –

one who strolls, one who is idle

well done, professor, have a gold star

even the amusement of the crowd

did not render Eugene homicidal,

so at peace did he feel in his heart.

He felt a sort of certainty deep inside:

he and Tatiana would kiss, within an hour,

an hour and a half, and after that,

everything would be simple. No more anxiety

concerning performance or rivalry;

she would ditch the audience, come to his flat,

and everything would be all right.

He would be with her,

be with her,

be with her . . .

Applause.

Eugene awoke. It was over. He wasn't too sure of what

she'd said,* but still . . .

    Confident, he advanced towards her, cleaving a way
through the crowd
        of visitors who waltzed this way and that, headed
for the exits, until
           they were left alone,
           but no:
Leprince too had taken a few steps in her direction,
        and then
she was surrounded by friends, in a hubbub of bravos and
congratulations.
But all the same, he noticed that Tatiana's eyes
kept coming back to him, as if magnetised;
        in fact, it looked to Eugene
          as if she were keen
            to get rid of all these others
as quickly as she could.
She thanked them for their thank yous

----

* That it didn't matter, in fact, what the young man was looking at /
that the fascination of the painting lay in its ambiguous gaze / the way
nothing was resolved, all the ways / it failed to make things clear / the
way it revealed itself by hiding / or hid itself by revealing / that art is
not there to *show* / but that it can / place an opaque body in front of
a window / and objects in the background /and yet speak only / truly,
only / of what is invisible.

let's have coffee one afternoon!
really nice to see you again,
                    yeah the thesis is going well,
        I'll tell you all about it soon,
        I don't want to keep you out too late . . .
all those things that we say to make someone go away,
            she tossed them out like confetti   to everyone
                    see you next time thanks for coming
        while seeming to check
        through the moving cracks
        in the wall of human beings
                        that Eugene
        was still there:
a smile at someone   *Eugene's still there*
a kiss on someone's cheek   great to see you, bye
                        yes, still there
a handshake with an American tourist who had just posed
a very long question   –
            an involuntary distress signal sent to Eugene:
            don't go I'm coming;   I'll just be three
            seconds   –   *thank you I'm delighted*
                        you enjoyed it
and then, at last, the biggest obstacle
                of all:

Leprince, who was strolling over

to her.

Eugene pretended to admire a work of art,

just for something to do.

Auguste Renoir, *Alphonsine Fournaise*.

What a godawful name
and she looks like a tart
why would anyone want to paint someone like that

Suddenly

the hall seemed strangely

empty:

a white cube mounted with

impressionist rectangles;

silence;

the mouse-like squeak of Leprince's shoes.

'Thank you for coming,' said Tatiana, 'although you might
have let someone else answer a few questions' (*laughter*),

'I'll   see you next Monday –'

(*quick glance at Eugene: yep, still there*)

But Leprince had no intention

of being expelled from Room 32

before he was through with his oration:

   'Remarkably articulated, exquisite Tatiana;

   Formidably fascinating ... what feeling, what fantasy!

What a fine way to start this beautiful Saturday . . .
Would you care to spend the rest of it – *ahem!* – with me?'
He coughed, noted Eugene, in some alarm,

> *Bloody hell, he must be serious about her*
> *if a smooth-talking toff like him*
> *can't even finish a sentence without coughing*

'It would be my pleasure,' replied Tatiana,
(in that instant, Eugene died)

> 'but I've already made plans to eat lunch with
a friend –'
(Eugene, resurrected, wondered who)

> 'he's waiting for me over there.'

Over where?

Eugene looked around: Tatiana was pointing
at Alphonsine Fournaise . . .

> no, wait! look! she was pointing at him!

She was pointing at him – and him alone – standing
in front of good old Alphonsine.
What a nice girl she was, this Alphonsine! He could have
kissed her two oily cheeks.

> Leprince had recognised Eugene, and looked as if
he was grinding gravel between his teeth.   He spat out:

> 'Ah, I see! Well, if you have other plans
> With, shall we say, other types of friends,

Then that is, of course, fine; see you anon,

If you still have a yearning for macarons . . .'

Dot dot dot

Oh shit thought Eugene

if he's ending his speeches with ellipses

we're not out of the woods yet, by any means

A fraction of a second later, Tatiana was there; standing in front of him, kissing his cheek;

he was so surprised, he didn't even put his hand
on her arm,

as he'd planned,

to disarm and arouse her

(he felt pretty disarmed and aroused himself, just at the thought);

instead he stood there, straight as a stick,

'It was kind of you to come,'

Tatiana said.

'Ha!' replied Eugene.

Not the most eloquent reply, got to admit.

He'd prepared several lines in his head – damn,
what were they? Oh yes, say how tired she must be

and he really didn't want to detain her,

but that if she happened to be free,

perhaps they could eat lunch together; ah, but,

shit, she'd already got the first word in, so what now?

'That talk was very good,' he said.

One more time with feeling.

'It was ... wow!'

'Thank you.

Are you free for lunch?'

'Yeah, absolutely.'

Worry about her being tired.

'You're not too exhausted?'

'No, no, I'm fine.'

'Okey-dokey, great, I'd love to eat lunch if you're not feeling too dead. But you should definitely tell me if you'd rather go to bed.'

Silence.

oh god no   *did I really say that*

'I will certainly let you know if that's the case,' declared Tatiana. Eugene, initially devastated,

that is not what I meant at all
that is not it, at all

chose in the end to find it amusing,
and they left the hall together,
Tatiana racked with laughter,
Eugene still cursing himself,

but smiling,

wondering why his life had suddenly become
a romantic comedy – a film starring Jennifer Aniston, say,
or a musical ... anyway,
one of those corny love stories
full of coincidences and hilarious blunders ...

and what do you know? Wonder of wonders:
it was raining outside;
might she by any chance
have forgotten her umbrella?
yes!   and him?   *no!*
Were they going to dance?
No, but she held his arm,
pressed herself tight against him;
six layers of clothing between their skins, and yet he had
trouble walking upright.

Conclusion?
That plan with the polar bear was doomed from the start;
he'd never have stayed on his feet, in all the confusion;
it's far too acrobatic, far too precarious,
too hard to keep your balance when you'd lost your heart.
You can't make love standing up when you're in love –
that's obvious:
being in love unsettles you internally;
when someone steals your heart, they also steal

                        your centre of

                                   gravity.

                                *****

They continued to walk.

        'Do you know anywhere around here?'

        'Yes, on Rue de Seine there's a sandwich place
that plays opera all the time.'

                                'Fair enough.'

They spied on each other as they checked out the menu.

Eugene ordered first – vegetarian option.

        'Are you vegetarian?'

        'No, but that sandwich looks nice.'

and more to the point I didn't know if you were, so it
seemed like a bad idea

        to chew up half a little piggy

                while you looked on, completely grossed out

Both of them carefully avoided

the hummus that gives you garlic breath,

        the raw pepper that makes you fart,

        the evil multinational Coca-Cola,

the pesto that leaves green leaves all over your smile,

        and the tuna, probably caught

while collaterally damaging dozens of dolphins;
amazing the number of questions we ask ourselves these
days that we didn't give a toss about when we were
fifteen – a kebab, a Sprite, and we'd end the evening doing
smelly burps in someone's messy room

   this, by contrast, was very civilised: ethical
choices and tasteful music

      (currently *Lakmé* – the flower duet).

  They went over to sit on fake leather armchairs:
thigh-squeak and paper-rustle as they unfolded

   their fifteen-euro sandwiches

   and examined them

   with interest:

      his was asparagus

   and grana padano;

   hers was tomato/mozzarella/prosciutto.

Each took a bite; how to start?

So what have you been up to for the last ten years?

  As the flower duet reached its climax, Eugene
remembered an old French pop song:

    you can't put ten years on the table

    like you spread out your letters in Scrabble

Sad but true.

  Thankfully, Tatiana

162

began the conversation,
guiding it by remote control towards a certain piece of
information.

'You've never been to this place?'   'No.'
'Do you live far from here?'

                'In the ninth arrondissement,
                behind the Grévin Museum –
                    you know, where
                    the waxworks are?
         I bought a small apartment there last year.'
'Wow, how'd you manage that? Buying an apartment in
Paris! The prices are crazy . . .'
                (property-price digression necessary
                for the remote-control guidance)
'Oh, it's hardly even an apartment – just a glorified studio,
an attic room. You're welcome to come and see it if you like.'
She nodded as she chewed.

that means he probably lives alone   *>>> dig deeper:*
'Do you have a roommate?'   'No.'
'So you   *(chewing)*
(casually)   live alone then?'

     'Yep, I'm on my own.'   *But alone because he's single*
or because his girlfriend's somewhere else? 'It's cool to
have no ties,'   she added, a gentle prod

in the right direction.   A nod
to the information   she required.
                    Girlfriend or no girlfriend
          and if he has a girlfriend, is it an open relationship?
                    So many things to be clarified.
                    He had fun secretly staring
                    at her green distorted face
through his bottle of San Pellegrino (he didn't like to drink
from the glass)
as *La Traviata* hushed
and Tatiana blushed
a slightly darker shade of green;
                    as if Eugene had guessed her question
                    but wanted to hear her ask it,
                    he did some prodding of his own:
'No ties? Well, it depends what you mean by that.'
          'I don't know ...   I mean,
do you have a dog, for example, or,   you know ...
um, I don't know,   just something   that you're
tied to, you know? that means you can't be ...   er ...'
                    He's doing it on purpose she thought
                    he wants to make me say the words
'I do have a job though,' pointed out Eugene
                    and yes I know that that's not what you mean

164

'A job, sure, but that's not what I mean,'
and her subtle remote-control guidance system guided
the conversation   *crash*
straight into a wall.

              'I mean other kinds of ties
              like
          I don't know, do you have
          a girlfriend, for example?'
Eugene savoured his victory, smiling into the neck
of his bottle of San Pellegrino.

             'No,
no girlfriend.   Is that what you mean by a tie?
             I mean, it's not the kind of tie that I
             would have a problem with, personally.'
'Ah, right.'
She was happy and embarrassed:
          happy that he was single,
          embarrassed that she'd had to be so obvious.
She wanted revenge, she made to leave him in limbo:
  I can't get a boyfriend anyway, I'm off to San Francisco –
  I might live there, post-doc, great opportunity,
  I might live there for years maybe,
     but something inside her told her not to tell him,
     what would be the point? To confess . . .

to let him know – what for?   Just out of politeness?
                    It was none of his business,
                    and it was still so uncertain,
                    and – and she'd rather
                    he continued to think of her
                    as freer,
                    she'd rather he continued to entertain
            those fantasies that she could see they shared . . .
But already Eugene, as if to make things equal,
was asking a question of his own:
'So maybe I'm imagining this, but is there
anything going on between you and your supervisor?'
                    'Professor Leprince?
                    What makes you say that?'
'I don't know, just the way he talks to you,
                    about macarons,
                    and so on.'
                    'Oh, that . . .'
'Tell me if you don't want to talk
about it,' added Eugene (illogically).
                    'Oh, no, I don't mind talking about it,
                    but there's nothing to say, really,   ·
                    I mean, he can be a bit overbearing, of course,
                    but nothing's going on between us – you know

what professors are like sometimes, obviously
he wouldn't be the first one or the last one to try
to pull a student, but from my perspective,
there's nothing there at all, honestly.'
Yes! Jubilation.
'So you sent him packing, in fact!'
'Well, not directly. I need his support for my thesis and
the postdoctoral research. So I just play the innocent, you
know? I act as if I hadn't noticed, as if it were just self-
evident that nothing could ever happen.'

Eugene was struck by how mature
she sounded now; how much more at ease
with boundaries,
with the desires of others,   and her own,
how after him had followed, he could guess,
so many men in her life, and she knew how to say no,
                when to say yes,
while he, Eugene,
                who slept with more or less anyone,
who never offered any resistance at all,
                was now writhing with impatience,
                desperate to know
                if she would yield to his advances,

                              yes or no,

                              no or yes;

he imagined her opening up to him,

letting him in

                              (this image flashed inside his head

                                    and sped his heart, like caffeine

                                          mainlined into his veins)

and then the thought that she wouldn't,

that she might say no,

as casually as he had said it to her, years ago ...

the thought of this made Eugene's throat clench tight,

        But the fear only lasted a second or two,

              and then he relaxed,

remembering that   he was with her now,

and that was all that mattered.

                        And he was not in such a rush

as he had been in his dreams, allowing their conversation

to take another deviation –

down a different path, winding, wooded, tranquil, through

forests and past lakes:

              changes of subject, changing points of view –

              they spoke about films and books, their families,

              their ambitions, about François Hollande and

              politics, their jobs, Ryanair, war and peace,

about Sasha the cat and Twitter and the new
Star Wars movie (better than the last three but
not as good as the original trilogy),
and as they talked they both felt confident and fulfilled,
serene and slightly thrilled;
they weren't walking on eggshells anymore,
but skating on nice thick ice;
this was a duet, an improvisation,
the harmony so sweet,
the segues so neat,
that you suspected them of having rehearsed together;
not cloyingly perfect, but joyfully alive,
with a rare complicity,
the kind that makes other couples yearn
for the same intimacy.

And, like you, I can't help but envy Eugene and Tatiana
sitting in that sandwich restaurant, by the window,
the view softened by a layer of condensation,
the accumulation of all their breaths and words.
I know – and they knew too, albeit subconsciously –
that they were experiencing, in that moment, a revelation
granted only to the lucky few, and even then infrequently;
one of those instants like a bead of mercury,

elementary,

where everything is simple, whole, perfectly right,

where all the parts mesh – the things that you say,

the tone of your voices, the crossing of legs,

       the nodding of heads –

       everything is in its right place,

       here in this clear, compact space;

       nothing could be added or subtracted

       without ruining the balance.

       As they chatted,

       they felt like two peas in a pod,

       Adam and Eve in an Eden where God

       had gone away for the evening

       and apple pie was on the menu.

Time passed, and the restaurant grew dim

as night fell outside:

       it was only four-thirty – hardly late,

       but it meant that they'd been here,

       the two of them,

       for three and a half hours.

They realised at last when a waitress came over and asked

if they had everything they needed

               Oh yes, absolutely

       but it's true:

they'd been there longer than anticipated!

'Oh, maybe you've got plans,'

(suggested Eugene – or Tatiana, I can't remember)

'No, nothing, no plans at all,' replied the other.

'We could go for a walk if you like.'

'Sure, if you like.'

So they grabbed their winter coats,

wrapped their scarfs around their necks,

and went off for a walk like old friends – nothing to report.

Yeah, right.

I'm not fooled. Are you?

When we spend three and a half hours deep in talk

(you know this, and so do I),

we don't just go off 'for a walk'

without the pleasant anticipation

that – having left the restaurant

and begun our ambulation

through charcoal streets,

breathing little clouds of steam,

avoiding the glare of streetlights –

that we will reel each other in

with sighs, smiles and silences,

and that, at a given moment

(I know this, and so do you) you will

point out a Space Invader on a wall,
your hand edging towards
my sleeve . . .
So imagine Tatiana and Eugene,
on Rue de Seine or anywhere you like –
in your own town or in Vladivostok, doesn't matter –
doing the same things you and I do,
the same things we all do:
shivering *it's got cold all of a sudden*
where shall we go?
dunno,
over there maybe
Imagine them making their way
through the Saturday crowds
on this February afternoon,
the passers-by wrapped up warm;
everything is cloaked in the darkest grey,
but the wet pavements shimmer
with silver glimmers like anchovies,
and here and there,
reflected in people's eyes, are flickers
of orange and red from traffic lights.
Imagine the way they sway
into each other,

the tension   'watch out, there's a motorbike'
      when he touches her shoulder
      to help her onto the kerb;
               'I like your scarf' –
that old classic, always works,
      a stroke of the cashmere, vicarious caress,
and so they come to a stop at the edge of a bridge,
as they must, standing close, leaning over the water
               and into each other,
the whitish powder of the stone staining their sleeves,
ostensibly so they can admire the Seine –
      a thick sludge of cabbage stew
      revealed by the lights of the riverboats –
           So this is all very nice, but
           Eugene,
           (this is getting on my nerves now)
           (he's not a little kid, you know!)
           Eugene,
when are you going to invite her back to yours?
     I know, I'm working on it, give me a chance
hey Tatiana, would you like to come home with me
         for some tea

       or . . .

    no, too late for tea, that would just be weird

Thirty streets, ten bridges, four public parks,
eighteen thousand innuendos, ninety-nine jokes,
twenty-one almost-slips, caught by a vigilant hand

                                                    and
still they're just talking: no decision, no kiss.
How many miles do you plan to walk before you say it?
            hey, would you like

                        to come to mine for dinner tonight?
                                    that's it, go ahead
                                'Do you have any plans for dinner?'
                                'No, what about you?'
'No.'   'We could maybe go to'   – *my flat?* –
                                    'that pizzeria over there;
                                I've been there before, it's not bad at all.'
'Okay!'

                        Oh my God, I don't believe this.
Eugene!   *I know I know but*   but what?
                                    All it takes is two words!
I know but it wasn't   *quite*   *the right moment*
maybe
after dinner
I'll ask her
then

                At the rate they're going, dinner will never end.

174

And they've ordered wine!

A whole bottle? Well, why not!

These two are driving me round the bend.

What do you bet that they stay there half the night,

ordering starters, main course, tiramisu ... the lot?

This is what happens when we let our shyness

get the better of us.

This is what happens, too,

when everything seems so obvious

that it becomes almost superfluous

to jump through all the hoops;

it's as if we've done it so many times before,

from the first unzipped zip to the quiet kissing after;

in fact, it's funny how well we seem to know each other,

so why bother

rushing to bed

when we could just stay here

and chat instead?

We've already slept together a thousand times

in our heads.

well yeah that's kind of true but still

I would quite like to take her back to my flat

in reality, you know?

ah, there you are, Eugene! woken up, have you now?

Is the alcohol doing its job at last?

go on, then, give it a try

'Would you like'   *to come back to my place*

'. . . a limoncello to digest?'

'Sure, with pleasure.'

Seriously, how much pleasure are you going to take

if the love you make is unmade by the lake

of alcohol you've both consumed

and the two of you are too drunk to stay awake?

And two limoncellos, two! The yellow leaves them mellow

and now,

as the evening finally approaches its end,

I hear two tambourines pounding faster,

shaking and vibrating inside their chests.

Tatiana and Eugene, even tipsier than before,

even more drawn

to each other, cheeks swollen and warm,

eyes sparkling, exchanged smiles

a little shyer than before,

a little tongue-tied.

The moment had arrived.

'Tatiana,' Eugene finally said.

It was the first time he had pronounced her name

(and there's no greater turn-on than hearing your
name in the mouth of the one you desire)
      'I was wondering . . .

I was wondering if you'd like to come back to my flat
for a drink?' he enquired.
               Well, obviously she would,
                of course she'll say yes,
                         won't she?

She hesitates, pushes back
a strand of hair behind her ear –
girls do that;
you know what girls are like!
      They like to draw out the suspense.

Come on, Tatiana. Put your hand on his.
Say yes. You will, won't you?
               How I would if I were in your place!
Don't be a tease – look at his face! –   she speaks!
     'Listen, Eugene,'   go ahead, I'm all ears
'there's still something we haven't talked about'
                  you can tell me later
'there's a subject we've avoided.'
She sits back in her chair, clears her throat.
                 oh please God no

Eugene's fears rise up inside him.   *don't tell me she wants*
to talk about what
I said to her that time, is she going to bring that up now,
and bring me down to size, just when everything's going
perfectly, when it's absolutely imperative that I kiss her
along the insides of her thighs?
Eugene: 'Oh, really? What do you . . .'
'You know what I mean,' said Tatiana to Eugene.
'We need to talk about Lensky.'
'Lensky?'
Lensky? What the fuck!

Eugene starts to hyperventilate.
This is not how things were supposed to go,
not at all. And they were going so great!
If anything, he thinks he'd have preferred
to talk about what happened between the two of them;
he'd rather get down on his knees, however absurd,
and apologise for the past, declare his love, and then . . .
Lensky!   *no, please*
I've got nothing to say   *I can't remember*
'We never talked about it, Eugene,
we never knew what really went on,
Olga and I. It's hard . . . I mean,

we still don't know –

you're the only one who does.

You have to tell me what happened, Eugene.

I need the truth.

What happened that night when Lensky fell from the roof?'

So that's it, he's screwed.

He's going to have to explain it all.

Eugene must return to the past

so the present can move on. That's how life is sometimes.

Memories, surging from the depths of a distant before,

can turn your now to later.

So back we go.

Say goodbye to Place Saint-Sulpice – and not another word.

It's time to return to 2006,

and our leafy Parisian suburb.

4

Fifteen years old!

Sangria, sobs, Shakira on the stereo.

Tatiana bobs for fruit – apple cubes like boozy
sponges – in a tub of blood-red liquid.

Fifteen, what an awful number!

She didn't want a party.

It was Olga who insisted. 'Come on, sis, don't get annoyed,

but it's true – you hardly ever have any fun!

You're only fifteen once in your life,

so let your hair down, enjoy it!'

Enjoy it!

If she were still speaking to Eugene, Tatiana could moan:

'My sister's been nagging me again to *enjoy* my youth.'

They'd exchange a knowing look.   Oh! –

How it hurts her heart just to think about the truth:

she no longer speaks

to Eugene,
after what he told her the other day
(no time to go into the details now)
(we'll get to that later);
because of all the dreams that he confiscated;
he locked away
her first fourteen years
and threw away the key.
he slammed the door on my heart
he laughed at the thought   of all her hopes gored
she hates him now   (if hate means adore)
he's all she thinks about during this party
of course.

And so Tatiana is present
and yet absent
for her own big birthday bash
in the garden decorated by Olga
with glass tealight holders,
with Chinese lanterns that send the bats
into a frenzy of swoops and squeaks,
with a big banner that reads

HAPPY BIRTHDAY TATIANA

with helium balloons in the shape of spermatozoa
        straining towards the dark sky.
The party is like something from a Hollywood movie,
        a sweet sixteen in California,
        not a failed fifteen in grey Paris.
Twenty-five guests! Olga's insane. Twenty-five!
Tatiana is not even sure she knows them all; there are
cousins, school friends, neighbours' kids and freeloaders;
        it would come as no surprise
        if she were to discover
        that some of them have been rented by the hour.
'Ah, Tania, Tania,' sing-songs Olga. 'Still lost in a trance . . .
        doesn't this music make you want to dance?'
                She grabs her sister by the hand
                and drags her towards the floor,
                but no chance;
                Tatiana shakes her head, blurts out 'Stop!',
                Olga blows her top:
'Jesus, you can't even stop sulking in the middle of a party,
                what the hell is wrong with you?
You're driving me nuts!
                All you ever do is read your stupid books
                and stand on your balcony

sighing like Juliet all the bloody time!
Girl, get a grip! Your life's not that bad.
Look around at all the friends you have!

Everyone loves you . . .'

Yeah, everyone *except* . . .
Everyone *but not* . . .
(etc.)

So thinks Tatiana, grumpy and glum,
the only non-dancer among
the bouncing bodies
of her friends from school.

But let's leave Tatiana to her misery.
There's nothing very original about her huff;
you can imagine it for yourself well enough.
And besides when she's in this mood, she's kind of meh;
I prefer her when she's frolicking in fantasies.
So let's move on to the character who interests us today:

Lensky.

What is he like, Lensky? A good-looking lad,
full of life and love, mostly happy,

rarely sad.

In the house next door, he's getting ready:
                    peacock-blue T-shirt from H&M,
black jeans, grey Bensimon shoes ...   I really like him
                    at this moment,
as he pauses in front of the mirror
to check out his reflection
and adjusts his hair like he's making a correction
to an essay or something. He's seventeen,
but he's the youngest boy in the world.

                                        Compared to Eugene,
he's like a puppy.

            Look in his eyes – so passionate and tender,
so carefree and happy – those big dark eyes
set under

            his eyebrows, raised in permanent surprise,
and around them, freckles like satellites;
his fine skin, draped over that light, slender jaw
(his bones look like they're made of bamboo);

            a boy-scout smile, always prepared,
if anyone is in need.

            That's Lensky. He cared.

            That's how I remember him:

a big little boy, kind and funny and sweet
and a little bit lost,
always chewing over a poem,
testing it in his mouth with his eternal menthol gum.
'Are you sure you don't want to come?'
he shouts from the bottom of the stairs
to Eugene.
'I already told you.'
'Tatiana would be glad
to see you, don't you think?'
'No, I don't.'
'Okay, as you like. See you later . . .'
and as he leaves, he whistles a tune
by John Denver: 'Leaving on a Jet Plane'.

Eugene, right then, bristles   as his friend whistles;
he's extremely   irritated.
For the past few days, since what happened with Tatiana,
he's been –.   how can I put this?
I'm not saying that what he feels is guilt, exactly,
or even that he's upset,
but he's certainly on edge,
less tolerant towards those who are madly in love.
Before, he used to smile at Lensky's enthusiasms,

but today,

honestly, he feels like punching the prat, with his lyricism

and his stupid teenage romantic love,

    which is doomed to fail,

        obviously; how can he not see, the cretin,

that a few months from now, Olga will dump him?

Either that or Lensky will get tired

of her – that's always how love ends, you see.

                Hell, what does he expect?

To write her sonnets for the rest of his life?

Bloody Lensky,

                  he's like Prince Charming on ecstasy!

Memories flood back through Eugene's brain:

even when they first met, aged thirteen,

on a video game forum, even then,

Lensky was the sucker

fantasising over Lara Croft, insisting

        no, I don't want to shag her;

        what I want is to marry Lara

        and live in the Croft family manor with her.

    FFS, virgin, go play the Sims,

        or Carmen Sandiego

        or some shit like that,

go build your little town on SimCity, that's what innocent
idiots do,
      wankers like you
            who only want to show their dick
to one girl in the whole wide world! You make me sick . . .

      And yet, at the time, Eugene had not said that.
He'd been struck, at thirteen,
by the lines of poetry that Lensky
used as his email signature,
by the strange genius of this green gamer.
They'd met in real life, and become friends.
      Lensky had lots of friends,
      but Eugene was number one – the enigmatic,
brilliant best friend, destined to be famous;
      Lensky was flattered that this guy even liked
him. He admired Eugene like an older brother.
      Eugene, a little smug in his superiority,
         had, over time, perhaps forgotten
      that Lensky was, in fact,
      the only real friend he'd ever had.

So there you go.   The person annoying Eugene no end
          today is his only friend.

He feels a sort of nihilistic urge, a desire to smash
something to pieces,

> preferably something pretty: a delicate toy,
> a little pink seashell,
> one of those things whose presence in the world
> increases its beauty, its worth,
> the kind of thing you'd have to be crazy to want
> to destroy,

something that would crunch beneath his soles
when he crushed it into the earth.

That is how it all begins:
This urgent lust for crushing beautiful things.

> From that point on, you know it won't end well.

Eugene is not his normal self.

> He's in the kind of mood where he thinks *fuck
> I'm bored what the hell is their problem all those twats it
> makes me want to screw everything up just to see the look
> on their faces* – those kinds of thoughts.

It's nearly midnight.
He puts on his trousers and leaves the house.

The garden gate sings on its hinges.   Tatiana hears.
She knows who it is, sight unseen: the gate only makes
that music when pushed by Eugene.   It's his theme.
Is he there to apologise, to ask her to dance?
He approaches, steers

    his way towards her

        and he's near

           when Olga pours her

              another glass of vodka.
He swaggers across the lawn, and she thinks

        she's going to sink

        into the ground
when there's a scream: 'Eugene!'
It's Olga, whom he kisses on the cheek
– no kiss for Tatiana, who stands there looking meek –
'I thought you'd said you weren't going to come?'
'Well, here I am.'

    He carefully avoids looking at Tatiana:

    not easy, given that he's facing her.
His gaze flies all around her, circular saw,
as if he wanted to cut her out of the picture;
Lensky waves at him wildly   *what does he want?*
with the ladle from the sangria tub.

        'Hey, man! You turned up!'

(It chills me to see Lensky with that look

in his eyes,

so happy that Eugene had changed his mind.

Fuck,

I didn't think it would be so heart-rending;
I thought I'd be able

to describe it objectively, but seeing him again,
waving with that stainless-steel ladle . . .

it's tough.

And his best friend does not return his wave.)

Why is he blanking Lensky, Tatiana wonders,
and why is he blanking me too, and then, all of a sudden:

'You want to dance?'
Eugene asks

Olga.

Tatiana shudders.

Olga, a little surprised:
'Sure, if you like!

It's funny, I thought you'd have despised
the Black Eyed Peas.'

Well, obviously he does. This is Eugene.
Of course he hates that pap-rap cheese.

                    What the hell's he doing?
                    Tatiana wonders, sensing the danger
                        of Eugene's behaviour
                    tonight, and aware that whatever he's up to,
                        it has little to do with Olga.
Lensky, completely unfazed, claps and whistles
at the sight of his friend dancing with his girlfriend,
their bodies entwined;

            he dances with another girl, and the two couples
join together, switch round, then split up again.
It's hard to tell   if Eugene is enjoying himself:
                    his face is like a book
                    in a language you can't read.
                    The way he dances is weirdly broken:
                    cold, but full of jolts and tremors,
                    smashing his heels against the ground
                    as if he wanted to crack it open.
Tatiana watches him dance with her sister,
                    and a vague sense of imminent disaster
                    is rising insidiously
                    inside her, when suddenly

'LADIES AND GENTLEMEN,
YOUR ATTENTION PLEASE.
I WOULD LIKE TO PAY TRIBUTE
TO THE QUEEN OF THE PARTY!'

Tatiana turns, horrified. It's a loud kid from her class,
Patrick Triquet,
who's grabbed hold of a microphone
     connected to the stereo ...
         God, what a dickhead!
     'So I searched on the Internet and found a song
that's perfect for the occasion,' he says,
     then starts to bellow some stupid tune, echoed
by the other guests:

Oh let us contemplate
The beauty and charm of the girl
Who we're all here to celebrate,
The sweetest girl in the world!
Oh look at her radiant face
Spreading joy like Lady Madonna!
Let us praise the amazing grace
Of glorious Tatiana!

Fantastic. This is just what she needs.

Tatiana hates being the centre of attention, and here she is
surrounded by a conga line of drunken teens
       wrapping her up in this godawful tune
like a mummy in bandages.
      ... the amazing grace ...

Through gaps between dancers   behind the
laughing faces   she glimpses   something
strange   but   what's happening?
      of glorious Tatiana!
         just get out of my way
over there   in the shadow of the trees   she sees
     Olga and Eugene   dancing
without music   a slow dance in silence   but
where   is Lensky?
     oh
     he's just seen them too
   what's going on?
Tatiana elbows her way through the crowd
       of swaying singing fools
towards Eugene and Olga.   What are they doing now?
    Tatiana tenses, suddenly seized
      not by jealousy but fear.
Lensky's over there, a smile a mile wide

plastered across his face, a smile he has to feign,
the smile of someone in terrible pain.
'Hey man,' he says, and laughs. 'Everything okay?
Not bothering you, am I?'
                          'Everything's fine,' laughs Eugene.
'Really? Okay, glad to hear it.
And how about you, babe? Everything all right?'
'Calm down, Lensky, it's fine,' chirps Olga.
'We're just having a bit of fun.
God, you can be so possessive and uptight!'

                          (Allow me to add that this is totally unfair;
                    Lensky is not possessive at all; the poor guy's
        so convinced of Olga's love that it'd never cross his mind
                                she might be led astray by lust.
                          That's not possessiveness, it's trust.
And if he's jealous tonight, then it's the first time ever,
and you can hardly deny that it's justified,
given that Eugene has his arms round Lensky's girl
        and his lips   are only three inches from hers.)

Olga's expression is odd:
                    contemptuous, cold,
                    even a little cruel,

although I don't think she's too proud of herself tonight;
you can see it in the writhing of her feet.

Even now, I still wonder
                what went through her head that night, Olga,
                why, when everything was going so well,
                when she wasn't even drunk
                as far as I could tell,
                did she let herself be seduced
                                by Eugene?
                who she didn't even like, really,
                Eugene, who she thought arrogant and gloomy,
                why him, why tonight, why why why?
Maybe it was already coming to an end
                with Lensky, I don't know,
                I never paid much attention
                to what was going on between the two of them,
but I think that when people do something like that,
it's not just a mistake; I think that Olga precipitated
                                a break
that she saw coming, sooner or later.
'Wait,' says Lensky. 'What's going on?'
                'Nothing, I told you. Leave me alone!'
He slumps like a puppet whose strings have been cut.

'What's wrong? Are you tired of me?'

Olga rolls her eyes.

'Lensky, chill out! You're overreacting.'

'Well, maybe. Maybe this is an overreaction,

but I'm sorry, seeing you rub your miniskirt

against his erection . . .

I'm sorry but, to me,

that doesn't seem like the kind of thing

that I should take lightly.'

Tatiana tenses as this idea fills her head

(an idea she would never have had herself),

and Olga, as if to give her boyfriend a real reason

not to take things lightly,

kisses Eugene on the mouth

suddenly,

joylessly,

and, annoyed by this row

and the gesture it provoked,

Eugene bites her lip, his own mouth

twisting over hers, his tongue

fighting her tongue like two sumo wrestlers,

so to anyone else, they appear to be

locked in a passionate embrace,

when the truth is, this kiss

is sad and cold and empty;
it tastes of Olga's watermelon lipgloss
and the failure of this birthday party.
And when those lips separate at last, they each make an O
as if to award a score of zero
to each other.
Only Lensky watches; Tatiana, wise,
closes her eyes,
and when she opens them again, she sees
Olga and Eugene shamefaced beneath the trees,
and Lensky, looking like he's been struck by a bolt
of lightning,
repeating,
'This isn't real, is it? Tell me it's not real. You're not really
dumping me?'
and Olga muttering,
'Oh calm down.
Stop acting like it's the end of the world.'
And Eugene: 'Mate, it's fine, no big deal.
Here, take her back, your girl.'
Their bodies unlock, faces registering faint disgust,
a smear of pink gloss
under Eugene's nose.
'Come on mate, I was only messing.

You kept going on about how good she was at kissing,
so I thought I'd find out for myself.'

      Tatiana notices that Lensky is leaning on her,
or she's leaning on him.   Well, anyway, they're
leaning on each other   silently,

      in mutual understanding,
the two of them losing all their petals, like peonies,
my favourite flowers,
so fragile that when the sun shines on them,
warm, and the breeze gently parts
the petals until they are gloriously open,

     in a snap of the fingers they just fall apart;
plop,   and nothing's left but one small bald head
     and a little hill of confetti on the ground below.
Lensky and Tatiana are like those peonies, so sad,
     all their joy gone, all their love lost,
     after the briefest summer bloom.

      I suppose
some people are so dazzled by the day
that when night comes, they just aren't ready.

Tatiana, suddenly cold, just about holds herself together,
her thin arms hugging her chest tightly like a nut
around a bolt;

198

Lensky is too weak to even stay on his feet;
he crumples
to the ground, repeating
you're dumping me?
you're leaving?
Olga gets annoyed: 'Lensky, you're pathetic.'
Lensky: 'But Olga, do you love me?'
Olga: 'Listen, stop getting so upset.'
'But do you love me?'
'It's got nothing to do with that.'
'But why did you do it? I don't understand.'

That's what he says – *I don't understand,*
in a quavering, half-broken voice,
a voice that devastates Tatiana;
it's the desperate, despairing *I don't understand*
of someone who understands all too well, in fact,
and what they understand is this: no one is safe;
no one is protected from the attack
which comes just like that,
without warning,
pitiless,
merciless;
and you are absolutely alone

when the suffering begins.
Eugene, of course, has known all this for years,
and has made his feeling clear many times before
to Lensky, who really ought to thank him through his tears.
Eugene thinks:

It's over for Lensky: no more illusions,
no more sweet hugs or whispered sweet nothings.
God knows, it was about time that he finally faced reality.
And so, not without curiosity,
Eugene observes Lensky
as he falls to pieces before his eyes.
He breaks nicely,
this Lensky
who increased the world's beauty;
he makes a good crunch as he's crushed underfoot.

It might have ended there.
Lensky, hands trembling,
chin down, lips wobbling,
coughing and sobbing,
throat hard as iron,
gets ready to leave.

From here, there are two possible scenarios.

200

Either:	Or:
Tonight	Tonight
Eugene will pack his bags	Eugene will pack his bags
and return to Paris.	and return to Paris.
This won't be	He will feel,
the first time	for the first time,
or the last	and probably the last,
that a friendship	slightly guilty
has ended like this.	and bereft.
They will sulk	After a few days
into a stony solitude,	Lensky will call:
testy, with a taste of tears,	you wanna go to Mackey D's?
missing	and over their Filet-O-Fish
each other	they'll feel happy,
though too proud to admit it.	though too proud to admit it,
And after they leave school	to see each other again.
they will almost forget	Sometimes one of them will
each other and	make a reference
when they talk	to that evening,
about that evening,	because, y'know, girls
they will say that it was	are girls, but mate,
an unpleasant but necessary	what really matters
lesson in life;	are friends,
it cost me a good friend	don't you reckon?

but it taught me
that in friendship
as in love,
nothing lasts a lifetime
and you'd have to be dumb
to think it could.
Anyway, there are plenty more
girls and friends out there.

it's friendship that *oh shut*
up
and eat your chips
instead of talking crap
that Eugene, what a shit
Lensky will think
although, y'know,
he's still my best friend

Two possible reactions to this slap in the face;
       in either case, thinks Eugene, heartless as always,
       at least something will have happened;
              it will be *interesting*.
So he considers with a surgeon's curiosity
       this friendship laid out, guts exposed,
       pinned down like a dying butterfly:
       either it will be a museum piece one day
       or it will survive, miraculously,
       this brutal dissection.
But while he examines the pink flesh and pale intestines,
              fate intervenes,
       or rather the mob of partygoers does,
       gathering round, a few shouts, a few shoves;
       they're not singing anymore, as you might expect,

because the mob,

unlike Eugene or Lensky,

knows exactly what must happen next.

*****

And what must happen next does not correspond

to either

of the two scenarios.

Jesus man what's wrong with you?

you just gonna let him do your girl like that?

you a pimp and she a ho?

The mob has no intention of letting these two

just walk away or yield.

Look how proud they are! Look at their prides:

a pride, when visible, is bright red, it glistens

like a blood orange; it has to be peeled

to its raw flesh as soon as it's ripe

man if he did that to me I'd smash his fucking face in,

someone shouts

what a shame it would be to let these juicy prides dry out

when they're weighing so heavy

on the branches of those dark looks

that stretch across   from Lensky to Eugene.

you queer or what man

        it's fucking obscene, you know you gotta
  fight him man you
just gotta   the mob urges   *gotta*
     the branch is hanging lower   *you gotta man*
the air is growing hotter   *you just gotta fight him*
fight   the intense scarlet that everyone can feel
must lie inside the prides of Lensky and Eugene *fight*
fight   just beneath the cracking rind, the thin peel.   *fight*
     They're far too fine for the mob to let them just
shrivel on the vine, these two ripe prides:
at least one of them must burst open tonight
you gotta fight   *fight*   *fight*

So Lensky and Eugene stubbornly walk away,
   buckling like mules under the crushing weight
      of their swollen prides while their fates
         dance impulsively before their eyes,
           and the mob watches them, entranced,
             because kids are always thrilled to see
        what happens when you trap a wasp and a bee
                in the same jar.

And now?   What next?

After that, it will all happen very fast;
one of them will be at the top,
the other at the bottom
of the house next door.   What went on?
Tell me everything.
What happened on that roof?   O Eugene,
sing us the song of Lensky's rage,
the fateful rage that led to his fall;
sing us the final moments,
but the truth this time;
not what you told the police that night:

'I arrived too late, there
was nothing I could
do, no, nothing
at all. I just
arrived
and
then
I saw
him
fall.'

Eugene, ten years later; a new interrogation
by a new interrogator –

yours truly.

What *really* happened that night, exactly?

EUGENE I didn't push him,

if that's what you're suggesting.

ME   I'm not accusing you.

EUGENE You're insinuating

that I haven't told the whole truth.

ME   I'm not insinuating anything.

I'm just asking

you to explain.

EUGENE We left the party. When we got back

to Lensky's house, he said: *meet me on the roof.*

He went up there, and I followed soon after.

Up on the rooftop, he told me:

my life is fucked up, it's all over,

and then he jumped. There was nothing I could do.

ME   Start again. Add more details.

None of this makes any sense to me.

Dig into your memory, Eugene,

this is important. Take your time

and try to explain.

EUGENE We left the party. When we got back

to Lensky's house, all was silent.

206

His parents had gone to bed,
the dog was sleeping. The only sound
was the hum of the refrigerator ...

ME   Stop taking the piss, Eugene. This matters.
What do we care about the bloody fridge?
Tell us what happened.
Tell us what you were thinking.
Describe how Lensky seemed ... I mean, Christ,
I know you're not a professional writer
but you could at least try!

Eugene sighs.

 'All right.'

EUGENE   Lensky died
several times. Let's start with that.
He died several times that night,
the first time in the garden
after that stupid incident with Olga – the shock.
His childhood died in that moment, and I admit
that I was tough on him.
I wanted him to be stronger,
more mature. I thought it was his fault

that he hadn't built a fortress around his heart.
And yet I'd told him, plenty of times:
Lensky, life is not a bed of bloody roses,
it's not gentle or moral, it's not what you think;
there's no God or guardian angel
watching over you.
I told him that again and again.
He never blinked.
He'd just laugh and say: *Eugene,*
you're such a pessimist – why
is your vision of life so sad? And all the while,
the rest of us were forging shields,
flattening our dreams
on the anvil of reality. But Lensky wasn't ready,
he wasn't armed, when the attack began.
So, really, if you think about it, it was his fault,
sort of. I mean, he couldn't claim
that no one warned him. Well,
that was how I saw it back then anyway.
So yeah, when I saw him
with the light gone from his eyes,
I thought: one day he'll realise
that his sadness was just sodding
stupid, that getting dumped never killed anybody,

that it was a good learning experience, that night,
and that one day he'd thank me
and say: *you were right.*
I'm not sure why, but I have the impression
that I've always liked to teach people a lesson.

ME   Yeah, I've noticed that. We'll talk about it later.
EUGENE I can't wait.

So he looked at me and said:
'I'll see you on the roof.'
The roof was where we went to smoke joints, me and him,
blowing the smoke out
towards the Arche de la Défense;
it was where we used to open up our hearts
to each other. Well, mostly him to me.
But anyway,   I hoist myself up through the skylight.
He's standing at the edge,
arms outstretched,
teasing the void below,
that arsehole.
I panic,
I blurt out
'Lensky, what the hell are you doing?

Don't tell me that you're thinking
of killing yourself for love
or some crap like that!
It's the biggest cliché in the book
of sensitive poets, you dick.
I gave you credit for a bit
more originality than that.
Don't make me regret
choosing you as a friend.'
Through gritted teeth, he answers:
        'Come and join me.'
          The implication being:
        if you're not too chickenshit.
And I realise that the others have convinced him to fight.

        He's right on the edge, the abyss below;
behind him, the branches of a tree are silhouetted
like the antlers of a stag by the moonlight shining through
a puff of clouds. I approach. The roof is slate, not too slanted,
        but slippery. I'm in boat shoes,
        he's in Bensimon trainers.
        I'm the one with a better grip.
I say,   'I reckon you've had too much booze.
        Do you really want to fight me over Olga?

You know I don't give a shit about her.'

'I want a duel.'

A duel. That's what he actually said: a duel.

And I thought *I* was the old-fashioned one! A bloody duel.

'I don't have a second,' I joke.

'Or a sword, for that matter.

Come on Lensky, stop being an arse –

let's go inside and play Mario Kart.'

I spout stuff like that for five minutes or so. Let's settle
things man to man on Street Fighter, let's have a beer,
let's read

some Byron;

anything to get him safely inside.

It doesn't work. He doesn't budge.

He still wants me to join him out on the edge.

ME   Are you scared, at that moment?

EUGENE Honestly? No. What I'm thinking

is that the whole thing

is too stupid for words, and yet

in a way I'm attracted to it.

You see, I have the impression

that the universe, at last, is coming round to my

way of thinking,

that it's proving the truth of my great

philosophical system,

which says that no one loves us,

that anything can destroy us,

that fate is arbitrary and tyrannical.

I was very young back then, I can see that now.

I was so young, and a little fanatical.

Go ahead and take the piss out of me.

I was so young. So dumb.

ME   And so alone.

EUGENE   Maybe.

You see,

             thinking about it now,

             I can recognise that this duel

             was a duel between

             our two adolescent philosophies:

Lensky's idealism,   Eugene's nihilism.

Sure, that's a bit simplistic, but when I stepped

onto the edge of that roof,

and he grabbed me by the wrist,

what I thought was that we'd both lost:

him   because his ridiculous belief

      that lifelong happiness was possible

      had been kicked in the teeth,

me   because I'd always felt
          that it was impossible for anyone
          to die for the love of someone else.
I didn't imagine that he would really
prove me wrong.

          But when he fell, he did, and in the end,
he was the one who remained faithful to
his system.

ME   Hang on, you missed a bit.
        How did he fall?
EUGENE I don't really remember.
ME   Eugene ...
EUGENE His hands were holding mine
        and we shared a sort of dance
        out of balance.
        We exchanged a few words.
        He had a little rant.
ME   A rant?
        What did he say exactly?
EUGENE Seriously? You expect me
        to recall exactly what he said
        ten years later? My head
        is like a sieve. I don't even remember

what I said to Tatiana.

Not a word. Nothing at all.

I hardly have a single memory
of that summer. Post-traumatic shock, probably.
Anyway, it's too late.

I already erased all that stuff from my brain.

Very well, then I will take over, as we can't put any trust
in Eugene's account.

Knowing Lensky, he wouldn't just have fallen
like that, without a word.

He was a boy who quivered with words.
Before dying,
he'd have given a speech. About himself, about friendship,
about love,
about everything
he lost that night.

So here is my attempt at saying
what Lensky might
have said.

Lensky's Aria

In a flash   in a flash
in a flash it was smashed,   the flower of my youth;
     it had been golden, like all youth should be,
but the only things that made me free –
     Olga, and you, and poetry,
     and the sun and the spliffs
     up here on the roof –
         have been stolen from me.
What will happen tomorrow?
         What will I do
     when I wake up in bed without my youth,
ten thousand years older, but with no more experience,
         no more intelligence
than before,
     because boredom isn't wisdom,
     sadness isn't a life lesson ...
     I loved you all, you know, even though
     you sometimes did bad things,
     I loved everyone, yesterday ...
yesterday love was all I needed, love was the only thing in
my heart;
     my life was so beautiful, but you've ripped it apart.

Oh Olga!

Well, if it's all over, if the last dice have been rolled,

  if it has to end like this,

                      promise me one thing:

      promise me you'll tell her

      that I loved her more than anything,

tell her that I had so many plans for us two,

    ten million plans, and promises too . . .

      promises to keep and eternities to fill . . .

                      oh, ask her

not to forget me like this cruel world will,

    ask her to remember all the poems I wrote,

      how I loved her, and how she loved me.

Go ahead and laugh, Eugene – I don't care!

    Of the two of us, I'm the only one who really lived

all the blazing possibilities of life; I didn't build

a shell around my heart, not because I was unaware

of the dangers, but because I dared

                to risk it all;

    I was alive,   before tonight;

    and yes, perhaps,

    I was fragile, and naïve,

            but at least I was free.

                    And Eugene,

that suit of armour that you wear, one day it will collapse,
               and you will die inside,
               like I have died.
          Olga, it was for you,
          it was for you that I went unarmed,
          that I laid bare my soul;
          it was to have you as my lover
          that I delayed the moment
          of rearmament,   and then in a flash
                    in a flash   in a flash
in a flash it was smashed,   the flower of my youth;
          it had been golden, like all youth should be,
but the only things that made me free –
          Olga, and you, and poetry,
          and the sun and the spliffs
          up here on the roof –
               have been stolen from me.

               Was that how it went, more or less?

EUGENE I don't know. It's possible, I guess.
          But you have to imagine him saying it in his voice.

He's right. Imagine all of that spoken by Lensky,
in his full, warm tones,

      in his voice that had broken, but not all the way.
Imagine a voice like those words: gauche and grandiloquent,
   passionate and swift, overly lyrical,
    and in the background one of those electronic tunes
    that he used to record his slam tracks. Now go away
    and reread the text with that voice in your ears.
                I'll wait for you here.

               *****

                       All done?
      May he rest in peace, then.
He could have done better, given the time,
but he was so young that we'll never be able to say:
           he wrote something truly great;
all we can say is:
           he was a writer of great promise.

      So young, so young; so young that it's hard to say
      who he really was,
    and, therefore, exactly what it is that we regret:
    perhaps that unblossomed promise,

preserved forever, like a seed in ice,
never to germinate.

        Rest in peace, Lensky!
        Ashes to ashtray, spliff to smoke,
        we will remember the last words
        that you ever spoke.

EUGENE They're not even his words.

ME   They could have been.

          They're the sort of thing   he might have said.

EUGENE May I continue?

ME   I thought you didn't remember anything
          about his death.

EUGENE Just let me speak. I remember . . .

                    I remember
          that I gave him my hand. I thought I'd be able
          to make him change his mind.
          I wanted to drag him up the roof, towards the
          skylight, towards safety.
          But he wouldn't come with me.
          He pushed me first . . .

ME   He pushed you?

EUGENE Yeah.

          Although, thinking about it,

he didn't push me very hard.   I swayed.
He caught me. Then pushed me again,

                         but, honestly,

still not very hard.   Now, I can see
that his heart wasn't in it.
He didn't really want to kill me.

        The third time he pushed me,
I tumbled to the right,
down towards the night.
I slid; the slate screeched under my nails:
a sudden memory of my primary school teacher,
Madame Labatte –
it's funny what you think of in situations
like that.
He was standing at the roof's edge,
I was on my back.
It wasn't funny anymore,

                 and suddenly I felt annoyed by all

                     this bullshit; I wanted to regain control;
I stood up and I slammed my foot against the roof.

                                'Lensky!'

Just one word. 'Lensky!'
One word, that's the truth.
But when I banged my shoe down, I broke a tile.

BANG.   The noise was loud, and not
                  unlike a gunshot.   BANG.

                  And just as if I'd really been holding a pistol
in my hand, and just as if this gun had been
aimed at him, Lensky jerked, like he was
startled,   and then he fell.
                  He didn't even yell.

ME   He fell because you cracked a tile?
EUGENE I'm telling you what happened. The slate
                  smashed – BANG – and he fell off the roof.
                  It wasn't just a crack,
                  it left a massive hole in their attic roof –
                  I bet it rained in there for weeks.
ME   And then?
EUGENE What do you mean, and then?
                  Can't you leave me in peace?
                  And then I saw him disappear over the edge.
                  And then I called the police,
                  or the ambulance or whatever.
                  And then there were sirens and flashing lights
                  and someone told me he was dead.

We went to the hospital,
sirens screaming through the night
in the ambulance, and then, and then . . .
well, you know the rest:
his parents, the police, I told them I saw him fall,
but as for all the other stuff,
well I wasn't dumb enough to wail:
'*It was him who pushed me, sir! Honestly,
I swear! And then he just got scared . . .*'
Not the world's best explanation,
even if it was true.
So I lied, and that's all; now you know
the whole story. Are you happy?

> I lied. I should have said
> that Lensky died
> because he was a fool,
> because he messed up his duel,

I should have told them all that,
his parents, everyone:
your son died because he jumped like a hare,
probably because he was scared of me,
because I was too heavy for your roof.

> Telling the truth.
> It's always the best policy, right?

ME   And are you going to tell Tatiana all that?

EUGENE Sure, she asked me, so why not?

ME   You're so cold!

EUGENE Sorry?

ME   I don't know ... you tell me all this,

          like it's just a story ...

          you manage to remember it all without

          getting teary ...

EUGENE   No!

          What the fuck!   No, no, no!

          I'm not managing anything!

          And you're pissing me off with all your questions!

And he sobs, like a little kid. I have to admit –

                              I don't understand.

ME   But all those years ...

          All those years, when you thought

          about that night ...

EUGENE But I *didn't* think about it!

          I never thought about it at all until just now,

          when you asked me what happened and

          you wouldn't let it go.

              I had to forget it, don't you see?

It was that or go crazy.

You have to make choices in life, and I chose

to obliterate Lensky and Olga and Tatiana,

and the whole horrible story of that summer.

And as time passed,

everything that happened

ended up seeming

unreal to me,

        like a story that I heard somewhere.

        It didn't seem like me at all:

too much love, too much hate,

too much emotion ...

it was all a bit excessive for someone like me,

and I ended up convincing myself that this story

was just a novel

that I'd read when I was in my teens,

a novel I'd identified with, to the point

where it started invading my dreams ...

His eyes are lowered. I'm going to leave him in peace.

He has to tell Tatiana this whole story now,

although perhaps not quite in the same way

he just told us: we are always better

when we tell something for the second time.

So imagine this story better told.

I bet you can.

Now imagine Tatiana's reaction.

> She's bound to be upset.

is he/isn't he a criminal
is the limoncello blurring her judgment, how can she tell
> *is this really the right context*
>> *for a last drink*
>> *in his attic flat?*

No.

> He will have tears in his eyes, and so will she.

He'll be shattered.

> He didn't think it would be so hard to tell her
> what happened.

>> 'I understand.'

She will be shaken.

> She'll need some time to think about what she's heard.

>> 'I understand.'

They'll understand each other. It will be all right.

> He didn't murder Lensky.

>> Well, not quite.

But his friend died all the same.

And he rejected Tatiana.

He screwed up more than one thing that summer.

Looks like the boy who liked to give lessons

learned a hard one.

Oh Eugene!

My darling. How could it have taken you so many years

                    to understand

that protecting yourself from your fears

is no protection at all

                    in the end?

EUGENE Still here, are you?

                    You do seem to enjoy this kind of scene.

ME   Oh, I wouldn't miss it for anything.

EUGENE And telling me that I was wrong.

                    Thank you for the sermon.

ME   I'm teacherly sometimes like that.

                    I like people to learn their lesson.

EUGENE Do you despise me?

ME   Despise you? I'm only beginning

                    to find you rather interesting.

EUGENE Liar. I know you've always been

                    head over heels in love with me.

ME   Don't flatter yourself, mon chéri.

Maybe a little, but not much. Where were we?
Oh yes.

Now that they both remember,
  more memories will come. Of the worst
    of that past,
    and of the better. Perhaps.

We'll see.

Until then, they will go their separate ways,
for now.
There will be no pillow talk tonight
nor any of the fun that comes before it
    (sorry to let you down).

  But don't be angry, all right?
In the next chapter,
    we will find them again, a few days later,
    and the situation will, once again,
      have changed a little bit.

5

It grew colder and colder in grey Paris.

In the mornings, the gutters were furry with frost;
then the black night faded to reveal
a sky that was platinum, smooth as ice,

that flattened surfaces, turned façades hard.
Around noon,

it snowed. The white sky

suddenly

opened its eyes

and big fat snowflakes started to fall.
Paris looked fluffy, and a little more welcoming:

about five in the evening,

you could finally go out again.
Tatiana went out almost every evening:
instead of going home after working at the library,
she saw lots of friends, all over the city,

       sending out texts at random:
              'Hey Cam r u free for dinner?'
      'Hello Martin, fancy a drink?'
and if the answer was yes, she'd get an Uber to Camille
       or a metro to Martin,
or to Paul or Marco or Gabrielle or Zacharie or Farah,
       and they would crowd around little tables
and play Tetris with plates of tapas,
talking about their lives, the jobs of some,
         the studies of others,
      the unemployment of the unfortunate,
      who were thinking of moving because it was
      too stressful in the capital,
the huge wave of break-ups among their friends,
romantic carnage of the mid-twenties –
      even Stéphane and Laurine,
      who'd been together since school –
and all of this distracted Tatiana in between
                texts from Eugene.
Because,
     while at first they'd kept respectfully apart
     as if Lensky's ghost was haunting
     the space between them,
     as if the wind from that lost summer had

cooled their hearts,
as if they needed some time for the past
to trickle out of the present,
after just a few days of guarded silence
one of them – who knows which? –
had texted the other:

I really liked that evening we spent together
And oh the relief in the other's face then . . .
me too   thank you again for dinner
and the walk   yes   it was nice to walk around
it's good we talked about   what we talked about
good thing yes   I needed to remember
I feel like lately I've thought a lot about that summer
and so things began quite cautiously,
but little by little, ice melted,
ghosts receded,
death died – a little –
and they wrote more and more
until they were writing to each other almost constantly,
thumbs tapping frantically;
and they talked not of love
or the past but of Paris today,
and all it had to say,
because it was incredible, the number of things

that made each one think of the other:
each street corner spoke of their affinity,
each show they saw on TV,
that's exactly what we were talking about the other night
each image in their heads just had to be shared.
hey I listened to that song you
told me about. it was beautiful. did you hear . . .
today's special at the restaurant next door to my flat
is a calzone –
you think they're trying to lure you over here?
I saw a girl wearing the same scarf as yours –
how weird!
I hope she didn't steal it from you
It was unbelievable, how everything seemed glued
together by signs and clues,
countless little coincidences;
the two of them read the universe like a horoscope, their
destinies marked out in the happy alignment of circumstances.
on France Info they were talking about a new film
on the life of Monet
you know that two-euro coin you said looked fake
the other day
well the vending machine just spat it out.
look what I just found at the library

[photo of a copy of *La princesse de Clèves*]

Breaking news! A *book* in a *library*!

Forgive me for being a little cynical,
but I think they would be too, with a little more distance.
At that moment, though, they were ecstatic
                    and exhausted
from the never-ending surprise of being reminded,
every two minutes,
                    of the other's existence.
For now, neither of them dared
                    to suggest another meeting;
in any case Tatiana was going to San Francisco
in a few days
                    for a symposium, she'd told him;
        she had things to prepare –
                    though exactly what,
            she wasn't clear –
            and Eugene, so he claimed,
                    was very busy with work
(though evidently not so busy as to prevent him
sending her a text every thirty seconds),
                    so obviously it wasn't the right moment.

But to compensate for this,
Tatiana was more sociable than ever, hence all her visits;
she was more affectionate, more tactile, in a glut
of hugging and kissing, attempting to replace the missing

Eugene with anyone and everyone.
And yet, even at the restaurant,
she would never let go of her phone,
glancing at it discreetly between mouthfuls of sushi

to see what he had sent her now.
And then:

Okay, that's enough, I think.
I won't reply until after dessert.
Or at least until I've finished this drink.

Each of them made up little rules:
No more texts until tomorrow morning
otherwise he might think I'm getting clingy.

No more exclamation marks!!! My next
response has to sound cool and detached.

They invented complex systems
of punishment:

If he doesn't reply in the next ten minutes,
I'll wait an hour before I reply to him.

Her message was so short,
I'm not going to send her anything tonight.

Oh, so I don't get a text this morning?
Fine. No problem.
But he'd better not expect anything from me.

   But soon, one of them would surrender,
and then a telephone would vibrate,
    quivering deep inside a pocket
    like a small creature having a coughing fit,
    and all their reproaches would be forgotten, quick:
    there was a new message from him/her;
its light illuminated her/his face, and – miracle of miracles –
it was longer than the one he/she sent before,
    or more enthusiastic or less dry,
    or laced with ambiguities to explore
finding it hard to work today –
I keep thinking about something else …
    or blowing all the fuses
    in the fantasy factories
    of their brains
        yeah me too I just went on Amazon
           and bought a couple of things
       that I might show you someday if you're lucky
    or hemmed in with little hints of tenderness –
a *dear* here or an *xxx* there,
    like the sweet stuff at the heart of a *pain au chocolat*,

and occasionally, the ultimate treat, one of them
would risk
the word   *love,*   when they signed off,
          which with any other friend would be
          normal enough,
but which, like a sudden detonation
               at the end
               of an ordinary text,
left its recipient palpitating,   eager to raise the stakes,
damp fingertips racing in little labyrinths over the screen
to sign off this time with   *love and kisses,*
          and now neither of them would be able to sleep,
writhing in imagined versions of the sultry snogging session
          hinted at by that *and kisses*
          and everything that would follow on from that
meeting of mouths.

          In moments of lucidity between
the successive tidal waves of desire unleashed
          by each text, they would think
                    OMG I feel like I'm fifteen
                    WTF is wrong with me
          They felt as if they were each possessed
by a passionate teenager who woke them late

and refused to let them go to sleep at a reasonable time,
who directed their dreams and rewrote their texts
and forced them to reread a ridiculous number of lines
from old poems, etc.

     They'd thought they were adults now,
      measured and mature,
until this fifteen-year-old squatting in their brains
      took over their thoughts and – even worse –
sent teenage hormones streaming through their veins.
                  Eugene, more used to lust,
                      controlled his libido without too much fuss,
but Tatiana, rarely troubled before by such desires,
        felt uncomfortably heavy, uncomfortably hot,
        constantly moist in every fold of skin,
        slippery with sweat and other liquids,
        wet from the roots of her hair to her armpits,
        from the backs of her knees
        to the space between her thighs,
        and it seemed to her that every part
        of her body – her mouth, the tip of her breasts,
        her heart,
        the palms of her hands,
the back of her neck –   were connected to her vagina by
                  an invisible cord

as tight as the string

on an archer's bow,

which was plucked by the slightest thought of Eugene,

and then, like a series of bells, her entire being

would chime within.

Hot and itchy, sticky in places,

Tatiana's body was no longer her own; it seemed to rise

like bread freshly kneaded,

her nipples rubbing uncomfortably against her bra,

while – it seemed to her –

her belly was a soufflé,

her thighs éclairs, and she hungered for herself,

wanted to share

her flesh with Eugene,

dreamed of him devouring

her from head to toe,

and she felt

the hems of her skin

opening delicately

to welcome him in.

It was far from ideal, having these kinds of thoughts

in the middle of the library, or the metro, or the street,

but she had no say in the matter; even whipped by cold wind,

if she thought about him,

she felt herself swell in sultry heat.

           So it has to be said, she did struggle a bit
           to concentrate on her thesis that week.

Then the moment arrived when she had to force
           this adolescent body
    to pack its bags,
    so she could focus
    because
    she was going to dinner
    at Olga's house that night, and tomorrow
    she would leave for San Francisco
    early in the morning.
Tatiana had never been afraid of flying, but now,
      out of the blue,
      electrified by a sudden sense of fate,
      she wondered if she ought to write
        a text, saying goodbye
          to Eugene,
            just in case.

    I'm taking the plane tomorrow, just so you know,
      because if we crash or there's a terrorist attack,

it would bother me never to have confessed
that I've been thinking about you for days now
and that I'm happy you're back in my life at last.

As not all her reason had deserted her, however –
most of it, yes, but a little bit remained,
just the faintest trace in a corner unoccupied by her
teenage squatter – she held herself back,
and told him instead:

I'll miss not being able to text you for the next few days.
I'll send you an email or two though, of course.
And I'll tell you all about it when I get back to Paris.

Bon voyage he replied.
I hope the films on the plane don't suck, for once.
Love and kisses . . . Eugene.
She sent him love and kisses too, in response.

*****

Olga, that night, had pulled out all the stops;
when Tatiana arrived, she'd already given the girls
their little desserts in haste;

239

they'd both gone pee-pee,

and she'd brushed their teeth

with the sparkly blue *Frozen* toothpaste.

So all that remained was to give a goodnight kiss

to Mama, Papa, Aunt Tatiana, and all their cuddly toys,

and while Olaf, a string pulled from between his

bottom cheeks,

squeaked 'Let It Go'

to send them to sleep,

Olga opened the oven

and took out a large quiche Lorraine,

then she opened the door of the fridge –

covered in magnets and drawings, coupons for frozen food

and the form for the swimming pool,

a note from the school about lice –

and, on a plate, she piled various types

of cheese:

a Chaussée aux Moines

a Saint-Agur

a sad-looking demi-Camembert

then resuscitated a wilted salad with a vibrant vinaigrette

opened a bottle of Merlot, slammed a baguette

onto the Plexiglas table   *Dinner's served!*

And her husband, who was very nice,

joined them, his left ear discreetly turned towards
the news on TV.
Olga was an otorhinolaryngologist
(an ear, nose and throat doctor, in other words);
she took careful note of her sister's glittering eyes,
her glowing cheeks.
'Are you ill?'
'No, no, not at all.'
'You look like a glowworm! Do you have a fever?'
'I'm absolutely fine, I promise.'
A palm on her forehead verified this verdict.
'You must be stressed, then, or maybe just excited.
Oh, San Francisco! You can't wait, I bet?'
'Exactly – that's it.'
'There's a lot at stake on this trip, I suppose?'
'Yes, that's right.'
'Well, you look very happy anyway . . .
why so quiet?
Here, have some salad.
What's up with you? You've hardly had a bite!'

Tatiana, knowing full well how hard it would be
to hide from her sister the way that she felt – the waves of
horniness, the hot

wishes, the hollowing and wallowing within her when she
woke and walked and worked and hoped, every hour, the
worries, the wanting, the howling in her head –
at last gave way, and whispered:

'I met someone.'
She was going to say more – *someone from our past,
someone you know* – but her words got lost
in a swallow or a cough.

Besides, for her sister, that was enough:

'You met someone?' Olga choked.

'Well, that's not good timing!'
'I know, right?'

'What are you going to do?'
'I don't know.'

'What does he do for a living?'
'He's a consultant.'

'Where did you meet him?'
This conversation, like a staircase,
led dangerously to an attic of archives,
all dusty and mouldy,
and above them, a roof
that was   treacherous.

Cautious,

but no liar,
Tatiana mentioned some mutual friends.

'But he knows about San Francisco?'
'Hmm.'

'He knows you might just get a job there?'
'Well, nothing's actually sorted.'

'I thought your supervisor had fixed it.'
'Can we change the topic? I don't want to jinx it.'

'And how does your new boyfriend feel about all this?'
'Nothing. It's not like that.'   'Why not?'
'Nothing's really happened yet.'

'Nothing?'   'Nothing.'
'You haven't slept together or anything like that?'

'No, nothing like that.'
'But then how do you know . . .'   'Olga

                              Olga, please
                              don't pretend
                              to be denser than
                              you are. I just know.
                              You always know
                              that kind of thing.'

Olga nodded, glancing at her husband
who was stuffing his mouth with a Camembert bread boat
the way you might shove something in your pocket.

The affection in Olga's eyes
moved like an ocean,
waves crashing down on
this man who was listening
to the chirpy TV host.
'In that case,' said Olga, deeply moved,

                      'you know what you have to do.'

'Really? What?'   'Oh, Tania . . .
if this is true passion, if you feel that this is really what
you want, I mean, if this is the kind of thing that happens
only once in a lifetime, then you have to go all out!
You have to sacrifice everything for it.
We're talking about love. It's no laughing matter.
You can't mess this up or you'll regret it forever after.'

        And as she spoke, Olga contemplated
        this very nice man whose name was Anthony,
        who wasn't ugly
        and who was a pretty good father to the girls
        (well, not a bad one, anyway),
        who worked at a bank and who,
        feeling himself observed,
        unglued his eyes from the TV
very   slowly

by   degrees

                             as if   reluctantly

before smiling

agreeably

at the two sisters who were watching him,

one curiously,

                   the other less so.

'What do you think, hun?' Olga asked him.

             'About?' Anthony replied.

'Tatiana's in love.'

             'Uh-oh! Now we're in trouble,' he joked.

'So I was telling her that love requires sacrifices.'

             'Well, of course.'

'If not, she'll regret it for the rest of her life.'

             'Oh yeah, absolutely.'

'Whereas, with you, when you decided not to take the job
in China . . .'

             'I never regretted,' Anthony declared,

             'not taking that job in China.

             What would I have done in China anyway?

             Here I've got my three sweetie pies.'

He looked at Olga and their eyes met in a gaze as sugary
and shallow

as a stretched-out rope of pink marshmallow,
while on the walls,
the countless pictures of them and the twins
oozed gooey syrup as invisible violins
vibrated in the air,
and Disney lambs and fairies and bunnies
danced over rainbows and the happy pair
continued to stare
at each other
as if time had been suspended
in a treacly cloud of sentiment,
and Tatiana was so disgusted by the sound of the words
'sweetie pie' coming from Anthony's gormless lips
bloody hell if Eugene ever said that, I'd kick him in the nuts
that she wanted to say *no that's not what I mean*
you don't understand
we're not talking about the same kind of love
what I mean is
well, imagine an old love, buried in a trunk
a love that had been serious, dark, baroque,
as epic as the Napoleonic wars,
something impossible and sleep-disturbing,
not some cheap imitation love like yours
are you kidding?

she didn't want to be insulting,

but clearly there was some basic misunderstanding

not some crêpe-paper school-fête hand-in-hand romance

I mean the kind of love you read about in books

and it got worse when her sister exclaimed:

'Look!

You have to live it, that's the thing!

You have to live it, Tatiana, you hear me?

You have to live it completely,

thoroughly   resolutely   interminably   even

past the madness of the first few months.'

'What madness?'

'You know. At the beginning,

when it feels like it just keeps

growing and growing;

but you know, even when it all stops –'

'*Stops?*'

'I mean the madness part.

When you start

feeling yourself again,

and not just a big ball of desire,

it just keeps getting better.

The wonderful thing about really loving someone is that

even

when the first fires of passion have died

even

when the honeymoon is over

even

when you're no longer head over heels
– and yes, of course it'll happen –

you'll be *friends*,

you'll build something durable and tender,
a trust in each other;
that's not something your career will ever give you,
so don't even bother.
I'm talking about something solid,
that the two of you have built.

From that moment on, you're no longer living just

for you,

but for the other person too,

and for the children that you'll . . .'

The children! thought Tatiana, with horror.

No, seriously, Olga

does not understand.

'It's not that kind of relationship,' she replied,
'I don't think

that's what we have in mind.'

Olga and Anthony smiled a complicit smile.

'Not straight away, of course not; first you've got
those months of passion, when everything is hot,
but things will calm down eventually.'
And suddenly Tatiana remembered the day –

                    how long ago was it now?

                              seven years?

                                        eight? –
when Olga had brought Anthony home after their third or
fourth date,

          (he had more hair on his head then than now)
and it's true, they were –   or at least they
appeared –
superficially, to those who don't know, the way Tatiana knew,
just how wild love is when it's true –

                    to be, well, in love

                    (truly madly deeply, etc.)

                    in almost the same way –

                    let's just say

                    that the difference was not especially obvious

                    to the naked eye –

                    anyway, what I'm saying

                    is that this love, between Anthony and Olga,

                    did bear a certain resemblance,

                    a little, at least, to what Tatiana

felt now for Eugene.
Of course, she could see now
that it had been merely an illusion,
a cheap imitation, the kind of affiliation
celebrated in tacky Valentines;
she could see now that Anthony's sacrifice
had been a huge mistake,
that Olga's pregnancy
had been the end of everything,
condemning them to decades
of nightmarish evenings
of Sisyphean boredom,
him stuffing his belly, glued to the telly,
her going through her list of Things To Do, stocking the
(admittedly adorable) twins' backpacks with snacks,
but the strangest aspect
of all this was that, back then,
you never would have guessed
that the love they shared was only phony –
it seemed quite real –   and stranger still,   even
now,
even   in the farcical fiasco
of this mass-produced cheese chewed to the
sound of the weather girl's squeaking

in the too-bright light
of the living-room ceiling-lamp,
in this excruciating state of existential
famine,

they did appear ... happy   *odd, this –*
it seemed to Tatiana that they'd simply   *failed to*
                                                 notice

that their lives consisted of opening tins of peas,
teaching the girls to say 'please'
and picking up Lego from the carpet
because shit   it hurts   when you stand on it
          don't swear in front of the kiddies hun
          oops sorry sweetie pie
          oooooooohhhh I heard
          Daddy say a rude word
                    Tatiana grabbed hold
                    of her glass of wine
                    to stop herself falling backwards,
her Stark chair transformed to a rocking chair,
the black and white tiles a skating rink,
as she felt herself begin to slip and sink;   *no,*
I don't believe it, it's impossible,
to go straight from the sublime to the ridiculous,
from passionate lovemaking and transglobal backpacking

to child-in-bed-tucking and Blu-tacking
             pictures
             to the wall
             in the hall,
                 it's impossible   *isn't it*
after so much love and intensity
                 to talk about the weather
                 to be bored together
                          bored together
This phrase echoed in her brain like some sinister refrain
heard long, long ago.

             It turned the blood to ice inside her veins.

'we'd be bored together'   *no*

it's impossible
                 She felt a bitter melancholy
                 soaking through her,
                 something between sadness and hate,
as she remembered the origin of those fateful words,
                 struggling against the weight
of the past
                 it's impossible
he was wrong   *not that*   *not us*   *it's not possible*

252

well of course it is   in fact, it's even probable
         replied the sad refrain,
           you were warned, right from the start;
it's even inevitable.

         You'd be bored together, it's irrefutable;
and you know it.   He told you before.

         But things have changed! We'll be in love forever!
No, Tatiana.

         The ending has already been written.
           You'll be bored together.

And while these memories marred and scarred her:
         'It's worth every sacrifice,'
         continued Olga,
'and you work too hard, you always have.

         You just keep working harder and harder;
I know your work gives you satisfaction and
your successes make you proud,

         but watch out for the excesses,
Tatiana,   you know you're allowed
         to think about yourself at times too.
         Life doesn't have to be a sad ballad.
When it comes down to it,

         you have to live your life for you.

253

Anyway, who wants the rest of the salad?'

*****

She really had to get back home.
Her flight left early the next day.

'Well, let me know what happens,' said Olga, 'and I hope,'
she added with a simper, 'that you will introduce us to your
boyfriend one day soon.'

In desperation, after refusing the last piece of quiche,
when Anthony went to the toilet,
Tatiana attempted to reach
out to what perhaps remained of the teenager
Olga had once been:
'Don't you sometimes think your life would have
been better with Lensky?'
'Len-sky?' repeated Olga, as if those two syllables had
never before left her mouth,
'What on earth made you ask that?'   And she laughed.
                    It was laughable,   after all.
    To ask a question like that! It was mad.

                          It was   sad –
    there were better topics with which to end an evening.

Tatiana insisted:

'I just think that   back then   when we were younger,
it all seemed more intense,   your feelings seemed
stronger,
bigger, truer,   if you know what I mean.'
            'It's funny you should say that,' said Olga,
'because just the other day –'
            she stood up –
'I found my school journal –'
            she opened a drawer –
            'look, this is hilarious,
            look at what my friends wrote in this.'
Tatiana looked. Page after page, day after day,
            between *another bloody maths test*
and   *geography p.68*
            English find definition of 'Sunday best'
        were many impassioned messages, written in gold
or glitter ink, or in those inks that were scented,
            but which had since lost all their scent,
Olga I luv u so much best frenz forever
            ('That was Philippine,' said Olga,
            'you remember her?
            I have no idea what she's up to now')
and hearts made up of lots and lots

of coloured dots, stuck to the page,

and vaguely manga-like sketches ...

Beatrice + Olga = amour toujours

(Olga: 'I have no memory of who Beatrice was')

The +++ gorgeous in the Cou-cou City Club

'The name of that club means nothing at all to me.'

Olga kept laughing.

'Crazy, isn't it? We must have been convinced,

or at least a little part of us must have believed,

that at fifteen years old we'd already discovered

our best friends forever, our immortal lovers.

Don't you think it's sweet how important it all seemed?'

But suddenly she grew serious again.

'Lensky ... Lensky ...

that's a much sadder story, of course.

You know what his tragedy was, poor boy,

his big mistake? It was his blindness ...

you might almost say

his madness ...

anyway, his total trust, his absolute faith,

believing religiously

in those feelings we wrote in four-colour biro in the break

between History and Biology.

Alas, poor Lensky.'
Olga closed the diary, using a fingernail
                to smooth down a Linkin Park sticker
that was coming unstuck,
        and whispered to Tatiana: 'Look,
                you know, I do sometimes think
                about his death ...
                you remember how devastated I felt?
                But not because I loved him. No. Don't you see?
                It was because I'd *never* loved him, not really,
                not the way people can love. I mean, I did try,
                but I just never had it in me, and nor did he,
                for all his promises and poems,
                all his sky-high sentiments ...
                The truth is: we were young, and we
                didn't understand love yet, we had no idea,
                and he killed himself so stupidly,
                for a teenage crush.
                That's what upsets me – even to this day –
                so much
                when I think about it: what a waste, what a shame,
                to kill yourself for a love not worth the name.'
Moved by this memory,
Olga dabbed with the corner of her sleeve

at two tears as they ran down her cheek
and, eyes red, nose very white,
she hugged her little sister very tight
     as Tatiana tottered,
lashed by a blizzard of cold grey words
   boredom   *waste*   *teenage*
nothing   *promises*   *boredom*   *stupidly*   *crush*
   children   *sacrifice*   *boredom*
Olga continued to hold her in her arms,
comforting, warm, soft-skinned, full-breasted,
and Tatiana, engulfed in her merino tube-sweater-dress,
shivered,
     wondered if it was true, what Olga had said,
     if all passions were doomed to wither,
     if it was true that *we'd be bored together*,
     and all the while the scent of her sister filled her,
     a smell she knew so well:
          some Chanel,
          a costly one, dark yellow like amber.
          The same perfume as their mother's.
          One that comes with experience.
          One with no citrus fruit in it,
          no hint of summer,
          no chance

of an exit.

*****

Not for a second had Eugene believed
that Tatiana wouldn't write to him while she was away.
He thought *she'll write to me ten times a day,*
doesn't matter how expensive it is to send texts,
she'll use the uni wifi or the one at her hotel
or she'll go to Starbucks to send me emails.
He was convinced that she wouldn't be able to help herself,
and he waited, impatient,

      for the emails to pour in,

      detailing her adventures in that foreign land.

      And yet, the evening

                she arrived,

Tatiana didn't write. Eugene checked on the Delta Airlines
site that the aeroplane had landed

         yes, on time, without any problems;

     and yet, perhaps – probably –

because of the time difference,

                    no text.

The next morning,

                    no text.

In the afternoon, Eugene finally sent:
Hello, American girl, did you get there okay?

                                                    No reply.

A few hours later, he sent a second text:
I hope everything's going well.

                                              Still no reply.

            The next day, he composed a little email.
*Hi Tatiana, I'm thinking that maybe your mobile's not
working there.*
Let me know what's happening when you get a chance.
        Apparently she didn't get a chance.

            The day after that, he sent a picture message:
                of the Seine, covered in ice.
You're missing a chance to skate.
Still nothing. He let another day go by
                            and then decided it was time
                    to worry.
                                        This silence
seemed to contradict all the available evidence;
the two of them would be together,
it was just a matter of time;

    260

no one sends a hundred messages, each written in a haze
of love, all in the space of six days,

> and *doesn't* end up replacing
>
> their paragraphs with plans,
>
> their commas with tongues,
>
> their words with hands.
>
> > If she wasn't answering
> >
> > at this moment,
> >
> > it meant she was in a coma!

Nervous, he wrote to Leprince.

Dear Sir,
I'm sorry to bother you. I was wondering if you'd heard
anything from Tatiana.
I know she's in San Francisco at the moment,
but she's not responding to my messages, and I wanted to
make sure that she was okay.
Best wishes, etc.

*****

The response arrived the following afternoon:

> How kind of you to worry, I must say.

Tatiana is perfectly fine; she is here with me as I write.
We crossed the Golden Gate together yesterday
And experienced an earthquake just last night.
As I'm sure she's told you, she is simply thrilled
To be in the city where the rest of her life will unfold.

Eugene reread this email ten times, concentrating hard
as if it were an essay in an end-of-year exam:
with me as I write   Leprince is in San Francisco?
                    I don't understand,
she never said he would be there, all she told me was
                    it's a symposium on Caillebotte
why didn't she mention her supervisor's presence?
                    And if he can write back, then why can't she?
crossed the Golden Gate, experienced an earthquake
if she has time for tourism,
                    why not write a text?
unless it's just a euphemism
                    for
                    we're having lots of sex?
Most mysterious of all, that last sentence: what does it mean?
where the rest of her life will unfold?
                    What the hell is he talking about?
She's only there for a week or so.

Hello Tatiana

I didn't know that Leprince was there with you.

I don't understand – he says that your life

will unfold there, or something like that.

What does that mean?

Send me a reply if you have time.

And remind me when you get back?

love, Eugene

Hey just a quick text to check if you got my email?

Dear Sir,

Thank you for your reply.

I'm trying to get in touch with Tatiana

about something in particular.

Could you ask her to write to me please?

Best wishes.

Dear friend, Tatiana is rather busy all this week;

We both have a multitude of meetings, I fear.

Tonight, we will encounter the museum's director;

He will be her mentor for the next two years.

Hi Tatiana

I don't understand why your professor told me that you

will have a mentor in San Francisco for the next two years?

Hello. Aren't you supposed to get back tonight?

Dear Sir,
I was under the impression that Tatiana
was supposed to return to Paris last night.
I haven't heard from her and I'm wondering
if the plane landed all right?
Best wishes.

We landed safely yesterday, at seven in the morning.
Hasn't Tatiana been in contact with you yet?
Everything went very well; an excellent symposium,
And the decision has been made for her next step:
She will return to San Francisco in early June.
Naturally, she is delighted by this news.

Tatiana

There's something

        I don't quite

                understand

what does your

        professor mean when he

                talks about your plans?

He says you're leaving

        again in June

                but that can't be right,

                        can it?

Dear Eugene,

Forgive me. I'm sorry for my silence.
My trip to San Francisco was brief and intense
        and important
        and I had to think things over,
        without your influence.
    I hope you understand.
Yes, I'm leaving. It's been planned
    for a long time.
    I have a two-year contract
at the Museum of Modern Art:
        one of those offers that you can't refuse, you see;
        a once-in-a-lifetime opportunity.
It was probably wrong of me not to tell you before.
I didn't mean to hide it from you, but when I saw
                you again the other day,
                the subject didn't arise,
                and since then
it's as if it fell through some secret trapdoor in my mind;
as if I wanted to forget its existence.
    But over the last few days, with the distance
between us, and all your emails, your insistence,
              I came to realise

that I had been trying to delay telling you the truth;
        I'd allowed myself to think of the past,
            too much,
        to wonder if it could all have been different,
        but I need to think of the present;
                of the future. And that future, for me,
        is like a new land
where most of the plots have already been sold,
most of the buildings already designed, most of the fields
already ploughed
        and I have to tell you that I'm proud,
        really proud
of all the work I've done on its architecture,
        and I know that it must seem terribly dull to you,
because it's not a grand adventure,
        it's a future that smells of turpentine
        and old books
        and dust
but right now I can't think of anything in the world
    that would make me happier.
I really hope you understand.
I hope we can stay in touch.
I hope that when I return from time to time, we'll go for a
sandwich together

on the Rue de Seine.

                    I hope that we'll write to each other
and stay friends.

Good luck, Eugene, and till soon . . .
              Tatiana.

*****

She's sleeping with Leprince,
    Eugene immediately deduced.
                    She's sleeping with Leprince.
    This American thing is just an excuse.
Like she just happened to go with him to San Francisco,
and   hey presto!
she suddenly decides that she can no longer
be bothered to reply
to all my texts?

                  Two-year contract my arse.
The two of them are having sex.
          Why bother with all that crap about 'ooh
I've got a big future' and 'ooh I'm so proud'?
             you're screwing your professor, you slut
He bit the inside of his cheek,

271

ashamed at having called her that

Look, it's her choice, okay?   *You're such a twat.*

Women have the right to sleep with who they want, but why?

       This is what I don't understand.

Why didn't you just tell me matter-of-factly:

I'm sleeping with Leprince?

Why did you have to invent all that other stuff?

What was the point exactly?

                 stupid b . . .

                 no, shut up

Christ though   *I really am idiotic*

              this whole thing is turning me neurotic

Christ   *how could I have let myself be taken in*

             when I'm usually so rational,

so independent,   *so reasonable,*   *so*

                  alone

The pain seized his throat like a dog's jaws

    and didn't let go or relax the pressure

    enough to let him   breathe   or drink or eat

    he just sat there, gasping for air,

    rigid with rage in his seat,

and in the days that followed, his mind worked through

various scenarios, allowing him to question

Tatiana's true motivation.

She's sleeping with Leprince because
she never got over being abandoned by her father.
She's sleeping with Leprince because
she hopes he'll help her with her career.
She's sleeping with Leprince because
she thinks he'll ask her to marry him.
She's sleeping with Leprince because
she wants to have his children.
                    In fact
      thinking about it now   maybe she's already pregnant
she was wearing that badge, after all, and how
            can I be sure that she wasn't lying before?

Finally he moved beyond this futile fury.
Maybe in the end   she was sleeping with Leprince
            because she actually loved him.
                              Well
                              why
                              not?
After all, it was her right, after all;
                              why
                  not.   Let's be honest.

He has the right to touch her if that's what she wants it's
not because you personally wouldn't like Leprince kissing
your neck that it's the same for everyone.

                                        Let's be honest.
Even if the idea of Leprince's cigar-like fingers
on Tatiana's tummy,

            of his parchment lips on her breasts,
            of his drooping belly hanging above her hips
            killed him ...   Let's be honest.
            If she's in love with him,

                        that's fine. That's totally okay.
And so, armed with this noble resignation,

he reached the stage of   *actually it's better this way,*
                          it's not like I was really in love,
                        the whole thing was just a gigantic con,
            and, with the hefty trowel of this allegation,
            he built a wall with bricks of self-justification:

After all I   don't even know   who she is really
I hardly   talked to her at all   I'd never even have   thought
of her again   if it weren't for that morning We don't have
anything in   common really   I'm not going   to waste
my time on   a girl who I don't even like   who's not

even my type   I already told her no once before   I must
have had my reasons   Even if I don't remember them
exactly   It would never work   the   two of us.

But this simple deduction – *we got all worked up over
nothing* – wriggled in his hands and slipped between his
fingers, an eel of explanation:
his mind told him it was true,
but his body said the opposite, because
nothing was more real for Eugene,
and nothing ever had been

        than his guts wound around an icy steel rod
            when he thought of Tatiana,
      the impossibility of swallowing a single morsel
      of food,
    the possibility of sleep suspended above his bed
like washing on a line:
all of these things are real;   this rough, raw throat,
like swallowing glass,
this fly-buzz in his ears and his stomach full of rats,
    all of this is *true*, and your wall of explanations
    is paper-thin;
    it would crumble within
    seconds if you breathed on it – ragged,

panting – while you thought about her skin,

                      about your hands sliding over her hips,

           about her lips, poised inches from a kiss.

           All of that is true, and you know it perfectly

well; even the devil himself couldn't swell

           every swellable body part with blood, transform

           your pillow into a pin cushion,

           and fold your sleep until it fits inside a drawer.

           Come on, admit it – all this confusion

           is reality. It's the rest of your life

           that's filled with self-delusion.

*****

Eugene wrote to her to tell her all of that:

texts, emails, even a letter or two,

phone calls, messages left on her answer machine   *my God,*

                           what kind of loser

               still leaves messages on an answer machine

                  ugh, look how far you've fallen, Eugene

(Tatiana – I think that we're missing out on something –

think of – why don't we – seriously I'm happy to talk

about – over again – is it something I said – the Lensky

276

thing – me too I do think of it you know – any possibility
tomorrow – but you don't reply to any of my – you know
what let's not talk of anything serious –
let's talk of Paris –
love and kisses)

But none of this made it past the borders of his mind,
and soon all that remained was the sadness
which enveloped Eugene like a cloud,
turning life and Paris a hazy grey,
muting other humans and muffling the city
in a dull fog of self-pity.
At night, if/when he finally fell asleep,
his sadness would be lying in wait for him at his bedside,
and it was the first thing he saw when he opened his eyes.
Still there, I see.

Good morning, pain.
Why wouldn't it release its grip
and leave him to breathe freely again,
untroubled, nondescript?
Why couldn't he just go back to the way
he'd been before all this?
before that fateful morning
when he bumped into her on the train?

That man he'd been – how he longed for him,
a little grey man – sure –
but not a man in pain.

Eugene wasn't stupid, of course,
he knew perfectly well
that eventually it would start to fade,
               this mist of misery.
Droplet by droplet, it would slowly evaporate,
be scattered by the winds of passing time.
But he wished the process would accelerate.
               He'd never even held Tatiana in his arms, so why
did her absence hurt so bloody much?
How could that be fair? All this agony, all this torture,
and not even the slightest touch
               of her body, her lips, that he could recall.
Enough!
It had barely been love
               at all . . .
     But the truth is that recovering from heartbreak
          is like convalescing after surgery;
          it takes time for everything to heal,
          for the soreness to subside:
          all you can do is wait.

He waited until April,
and he waited and waited,
but still ... not a single
particle of that mist
dissipated.

*****

Around mid-May, awake at last, the city
stretched itself and yawned,
spat a few birds back in the sky,
hung a few buds from the branches of trees,
and Eugene ventured out onto the streets.
Noticing the girls in shortened skirts,
he imagined their long legs
coiled around his waist like soft-skinned boas.
This idea, though lukewarm, did him some good;
it was a sign
of the happy numbings
and dumbings
to come
that might finally stifle
the screaming of the past few months.

It was too early, of course, to start hanging around in bars –
he was still surrounded by his personal cloud of strife –
but for the first time he thought there was a chance
that he might forget, at last,
for a few seconds, at least,

        that he had completely screwed up his life.

Forget that he'd killed/not killed his best friend.
Forget that he'd killed/not killed his only love.
Forget that he'd broken
every single precious thing he'd ever touched.
Forget all that, as shorter and shorter skirts

        brushed past him and he felt more alive.
        Not much.
        But a little.
        A faint, distant stirring of life.
So he puffed up his chest
and forced himself
to whistle. He knew it was absurd,
but he needed to know
that the inside of his torso
was not hollow, but full
of music, as yet unheard.

*****

Meanwhile,

    at the Sainte-Geneviève Library,

    leviathan of metal and stone,

    beneath the noble arches,

    among the students dazzled by the shafts of sunlight

that kept crashing into its windows,

    Tatiana was trying to concentrate.

    In front of her, a pot-bellied tome of paper and leather.

        Inside it, interminable paragraphs

        with no meaning whatsoever.

Transmogrified by the pointillist hyperthymesia,
the polychrome, coruscating landscape
overstimulates – one might even say, brings to
a state of synaesthesia – the observing subject.

        Damn I should write to him

    A book like a bucket of clams,

    sentences like flabby molluscs,

from which she couldn't extricate a sliver of broken shell.

        No that'd be a really stupid thing to do.

No.

Only two more days to go
you can hold out for two more days, can't you?

Degas's ballerina is, in all probability, soteriological;
touched by her messianic grace, we caress the
dream of a utopian and sempiternal weightlessness.

what the hell is that supposed to mean
why can't this idiot just talk normally

Impossible to make any sense of these cryptic phrases.
Tatiana put the book in her bag
and her forehead in her hands
and pushed her eyeballs until, beneath the lids,
there appeared Bastille Day,
the magical fireworks display
that we all have inside our closed eyes,
an entertainment for those moments
when we don't know what else to do with our lives.
been so tired lately and everything aches.
But even when she pushed hard with both her thumbs
and saw the grand climax of explosions,
Tatiana didn't really appreciate it.
God what's wrong with me?

Why can't I concentrate?

After having made her decision

in San Francisco,

Tatiana had at first felt   fine,

fulfilled, content.   Serene.   And then,

for a long time she'd gone to bed early, and slept

peacefully through the night;

she was going to cross the great ocean   without him,

without anyone,

because she had big dreams and that was all she needed;

and besides, after the whole mess

with Lensky, and what Eugene had confessed –

and Olga, my God! Olga and Anthony! –

well anyway, she didn't need to drag all that around

with her for the rest of her life.

The past was the past, and the future was hers –

And, weird as it seemed, it didn't involve

the man who she thought

that she loved.

Because in San Francisco she had seen

what she would miss out on if she let

Eugene

into her life: the beauty,

the true beauty

of the existence she had elected for herself,
examined and executed.
She understood now
which passions are destined to consume us
all the way through our long existence,
tender and glorious, never to die.
She knew without a doubt
that there were colours
and paintbrush strokes
that throughout her life
would glaze her eyes with tears,
and that kind of love would never lose its charm;
never in her life would she look at her favourite painting
and think

I don't know what I ever saw in you
or   *you're getting old*
or   *I wasted so much of my life looking at you*
Loves like those were no accidents,
a friend of your sister's boyfriend
encountered in a garden,
who only talks to you
because he has nothing better to do,
and whom you start to wait for
the following day

because you're young and lonely
and easily impressed
by his pencil-shaded art,
and because anyone, in those circumstances,
could just come in and break your heart . . .
                                             no!
Her own passions, the real ones, the good ones,
were long-lasting. She would stay faithful to them;
they were the only things that were truly hers.
And in San Francisco she had met like-minded people,
moved by the same enthusiasms.
And it's not as if there weren't lots of young men over there,
handsome and eligible,
and perfectly compatible.
If it came down to it, she'd be spoiled for choice:
a sea full of healthy fish
to hook and reel in
and she could always throw them back if the feeling
wasn't right.
The boys in San Francisco would read what she wrote,
they'd listen when she spoke,
they'd understand when she said
that the light coming through the curtains
in *Martial Playing the Piano*

was a miracle of precision
where did Caillebotte find that yellow?
it's like a mixture of butter and sunlight

                Oh, it would be tough, of course,
those first few days, those first few months
far from all she knew,

                      from Eugene,
but quickly, soon, she would adapt to
and thrive in this American life, this
New World washed clean
of all the problems of the past;
and after a few weeks, she would start to work seriously
on driving one of those young men
(glimpsed in the white space of a museum, inevitably)
crazy with love, and the two of them would concentrate
on nurturing
their tender, scholarly relationship,
to make it as efficient as it was delicious,
always constructive,   never boring.
It has to be admitted
that Tatiana was sometimes disturbed
in the midst of her projects

             by the sudden vibration of her telephone,
the rattle of castanets;

the messages from Eugene stung her, it was true,
like little sea urchins in her big rubber boots,

        but she wanted something new,
and before her the ocean stretched out, foaming and free,

        calling to her: *come to me*,
and so she knew she had to cross it, this great sea,

        to be who she wanted to be.
And anyway,

        the decision had been made

                already.

*****

Except that ... for the last few weeks or so,
Eugene's words
had started
to scamper
softly
through her thoughts,   to play on her mind,
though in truth,   they had never really stopped:
she kept on her person

        her phone, with Eugene's texts inside,
        her laptop, with Eugene's emails inside,
        the two letters Eugene had sent her,

neatly folded in her handbag, and
– most importantly –

        everything Eugene had said to her
        from the very start,
crammed into a storeroom in her heart,
or her memory at least,
and now the door to that storeroom
had been flung wide open
and all those words were scurrying over Tatiana's skin
with their light, soft paws,
    like kittens,

        the feel of their claws
        always halfway between
        a caress and a scratch.
          And now Eugene
hates me, for sure; I should have been clear with him
from the beginning

        She reread his last email

                  last
the word gripped her throat:
        Tatiana never cried, or hardly ever,
          but in that moment she choked
             I must be tired
hardly a surprise

288

I've spent the last two weeks packing my belongings
                                        and saying goodbye
to Olga, to Mama, to the twins

                        but it was those others who'd cried,
                not her,
                because, deep down,
                she was happy to be leaving;
for them, it was sad, of course, she got that,
but she was filled with the selfish serenity of a Marco Polo,
an explorer, the wind in her sails, heading out abroad,
                                        voyaging solo:
                the world's my oyster.
                And then, while loitering between
two rows of shelves in the library, it was as if she saw him
there again:
Eugene,

                intent on breaking the dreams
                that were supposed to carry Tatiana
                onwards into the future;
                Eugene, her ball and chain . . .
how could she free herself, how could she slay
this Eugene who haunted her thoughts,
this immortal hydra who, since the age of fourteen had
always resurfaced

at just the wrong time, in just the wrong place?

          And so, moping over the cruelty of her fate,
two days before her flight,
Tatiana fingered the keys of her new MacBook,
              sliding the cursor across the screen
                  idly, or so it seemed,
towards a certain icon,
        which makes me suspect
that she was in the process of considering
the possibility,
       among others,
       that it was not entirely certain
              just yet
that   the fat   lady   had already   sung.

              *****

     And so it was that, elsewhere, at that moment,
Eugene, who,
was in fact beginning to
feel a little better, his cloud of despondency
finally lifting, grey turning to transparency
and revealing the first dim colours

      in the world around,

         the first pale rays of sunlight,

heard, to his surprise,   the *ping* of Skype.

         tatiana.reinal

                      Skype announced

        would like to

                      Skype announced

      connect with you

                      Skype announced

In the middle of his screen, a little circle appeared
around Tatiana's smiling face –

         a photo that was at least three years old.

      And these words:

Hello, I would like to add you on Skype.

         (the automatic message Skype provides

         for those who want to add someone on Skype)

Eugene stared at the icon, and muttered:
'I hate you,

        seriously, I hate your guts,'

before immediately clicking Accept,
his fingers like lengths of firehose,

                       291

his body shaken by a Ben Hur-style chariot race,
horses galloping from the back of his neck
to the tips of his toes.

Trembling, he awaited the next step,

for her to reply or explain or justify or

shit look at that she's writing

the little pencil's moving that means she's writing something
he watched the dance of the little pencil as it moved

'the little pencil's moving'

he repeated in his head, like a child hypnotised

by an Apple screensaver

it's moving   *wow, it's moving a lot*

is she writing me a novel or what

thousands of words were being written at this very moment;

Eugene savoured

the thought of Tatiana seeking the right terminology
in which to couch her desperately sincere apology:

'I am so, so sorry, Eugene; you are the love of my life and
I want to be with you, come what may. Things went very
badly with Leprince; he refuses to marry me and he's
boring in bed anyway. And you know I hate my stupid PhD
and I want to leave and live with you somewhere in Siberia.'

The little pencil was still moving.
What on earth could she be saying?

Maybe:

'The only thing is that I am very, very sexually active and
I need to know if that would be a problem for you. For
example, it's perfectly possible that I would wake you up
several times a night. Would that be all right?'

Dear Tatiana, thought Eugene,
that would not pose a problem to me.
I promise to meet your needs and fulfil your desires
whenever and wherever they may arise.

The pencil continued its waltz across the screen,
and the chair on which he sat trembled under Eugene's
tense body; not that he noticed, for his eyes
were riveted to the pixel pencil as it scribbled
next to the circle with a twenty-one-year-old Tatiana inside;
he sat there waiting, and so did I –

        although I am in a position to tell you –
        because I was in both places at the same time,
        thanks to my somewhat mysterious privileges,
        that Tatiana wasn't feeling ultra-confident either;

she was in control of the little moving
pencil, that's true, but
just like Eugene,
she was shivering from head to foot,
constantly having to go back and correct
the typos that littered her text
because she was clumsy and overwrought,
and it had taken her so long to write all this!
All this! This enormous block of words that said
that said oh but hang on no
Command + A and then Delete
You've got to be kidding! I'm appalled.
What the hell has she done?
I know someone who isn't going to be happy.
Eugene, I'm sorry:
she deleted it all.

Eugene had seen.
Well, what he'd seen, in fact, was   the pencil halt
hesitate
then gesticulate
as it erased
the magnum opus she'd spent the last five minutes writing.
And yet, he didn't really react.

294

His face looked like it was frozen, in fact.

His stalactite teeth made a grinding sound,

but apart from that,

all was fine.

He imagined the unknown words swirling down the giant
plughole of the Internet,

vanishing into the black hole of cyberspace,

and he found a sort of nostalgic consolation

in this. It was just like when, in his imagination,

the sun would implode and swallow up the Earth.

What did she want to say?

Why should I care?

It's gone now. It's vanished forever.

He felt oddly soothed by this idea.

A few seconds later, the pencil started moving again,

before spitting out the following message:

hello

'Okay,' Eugene said calmly to his computer screen.

He wrote *hello*

and the pencil excitedly recommenced its gymnastics:

how are you?

Always ready with a lie,

Eugene replied:

great, and you?

i'm okay.

i wanted to wish you happy birthday before i want away

Happy birthday.

Given that his birthday was not for another two weeks,

this seemed like a lame excuse.

As for that Freudian slip . . . want away?

That meant she wanted him,

or that she wanted to stay,

or she wanted away from Leprince, perhaps . . .

when do you leave?

the day after tomoto

you say tomorrow, I say tomoto?

Let's call the whole thing off?

Or maybe not all typos revealed some

inner meaning, after all . . .

wow

are you all packed?

nearly

i've got two suitcases full of stuff

i hope I'm not going to exceed the weight limit

oh yeah, it's 20 kilograms or something like that, isn't it?

not that much for two years away, really

yeah exactly

296

what will you do with your cat?
i'm taking him with me
in the baggage hold, poor thing,
he won't be happy about that
but there'll be loads of space for him over there I bet
yes

And after that, there was a blank.
On each side of the void, facing their screen,
separated/bound by miles of electrical wires,
Tatiana and Eugene
observed each other sightlessly.
A blind date in the literal sense;
a mole staring at its reflection.
This is often how it feels when you find yourself
deep in discussion
with a smiley face, or a photograph,
                              or a small green telephone icon.
And below this, the words,
which often have no real meaning
other than the fact that they have been sent;
there's no point trying to read between the lines
because there's nothing there but white space; what's meant
is only to be found beyond the lines,

in the fact of their origin,
in the motivation behind them.   But what is that?

so

any plans for your birthday?

no not really
it's not an important one anyway

The pencil began to move again. It's true
        that this pencil could drive you crazy,
        but at least   it seems   to care about you.
        It knows it has a mission to fulfil,

                            this little pencil,
        and it does its bit
        to make sure that you know
        that you are not alone.
        Which is kind of a big deal, isn't it?
        The pencil soothes our abandonment anxiety,
        our dread of desertion.
        Its existence, symbolic of someone else's presence,
        allows us to see
the fingers of the other person, touching the keys of their
keyboard. We know, at least, that somewhere
someone is writing something

for our attention.

i'm sorry for my silence
Eugene
it was just that I had to concentrate on my departure
you know what i mean?

The word departure was a dart in his heart.

no no I understand

said Eugene, who did not, of course.
Then he added:

you know you can just tell me
if there's something going on between
you and your supervisor

Pencil. Pencil pencil pencil.

FFS would you give it a rest
there's nothing going on with Leprince
why are you so obsessed

ah OK
sorry i'm just an idiot sometimes
i get all worked up about nothing
i put two and two together and get five

but I already told you

yeah but it's hard to believe

> *i just have the feeling that there's something else*
>> *i ought to know*

well
maybe there is

Blank

Eugene i keep thinking about something
you told me once

>> *what?*

something you said to me on the stairs
ten years ago

>> *what did i say?*

Another blank

you don't remember?

>> *no, i forgot all that stuff*
> *i don't even know who i was back then well enough*
>> *to guess. so what did i say?*

Pencil. Eraser. Pencil again.
you really don't remember?

>> *no, Tatiana, not at all*

you don't recall

the day when you came up to me
at the top of the stairs
and you said

                              what did I say?

that's so like you, you know,
to ruin people's lives like that, and your own
at the same time, and to forget it all a second later
you said
Eugene you told me
you said that we'd be bored together

He contemplated those words, and suddenly
a scene returned to his memory,
          a scene acted out by someone else,
like a solemn soliloquy   heard long ago
in a theatre,
          in the almost-dark,
          lines spoken with an actor's art,
                    perfect for the part,
admittedly,
          but without any poetry
                    or any heart . . .

6

... in which a character a bit like him had said:

EUGENE

You wrote to me, Tatiana, there's no point saying you didn't. You wrote to me and your message was actually quite well-written.

It had a sort of rhythm, a certain poetic feel, of which I approved. In fact, I was even quite moved. You know that I like you. You're like a sister to me, or maybe even ... yes, maybe even more than that. So yes, we get on well, and if I was looking for someone, then, sure, I'd wait until you weren't a child anymore, but I would have no difficulty thinking of the sweetness of shared moments, here in Paris – or even somewhere else – with you. Why not, after all?

But I'm afraid that is not the case. I am not of a disposition that encourages affection. I rarely even think about such things. They don't really interest me, in fact. When you have had as many love affairs as I've had, you'll understand. It's interesting to begin with, but you soon grow weary of it. The *khandra* crushes you in its tedious grip. Even if I was in love with you, after a while I'd get bored.

We'd get bored.

Tatiana, we'd be bored together.

Maybe that sounds sad, but it's the truth. I still haven't found a remedy for the ills of existence, but if one does exist, I suspect that love is not one of the main ingredients. I hope you won't be upset if I tell you this: that you're still a kid, and that I know – unlike you – what love is, and what it's not. And even if your feelings were what you imagine they are, they're not worth a lot. You don't fall in love like that just because fate presents you with a handsome face glimpsed over a garden gate.

Thank you for your message. However, love is not what it seems. The truth is we'd be bored.

We'd be bored together.

Exit Eugene.

7

We're such idiots in our teens.
Well, no. Not all of us. Not them. Not Tatiana or Lensky.
                                Just me, Eugene.
Lensky was in love   *he was right*
Tatiana was in love   *she was right*
                        They were mature
                        beyond their years,
        while I, so elegant, blasé and decadent,
                so damn incapable of sentiment,
                        I was nothing but an idiot.
Lensky and Tatiana understood;
I thought they were naïve, but in reality
        the naïve one was me –
I loved you both, you know,
even though you sometimes did bad things
        – and I who didn't love anyone, I who needed so badly

to be loved,

    I drove them away, one after another.

    I let them abandon me.

    Oh, Lensky,

                              oh Tatiana,

  all along

      you were right

      and I was wrong.

      I thought I was so mature;

      I felt sure

      I couldn't go wrong as I planted

      the flower of my future

      in the most arid soil I could find,

      the least fertile, because

      I didn't want my life to be too easy

      or too beautiful . . .

                  shit, I was blind!

                I was wrong all along

                  and they were right,

and they did their best to make me a better man.

      I mean,

      I was seventeen!

    Why did I have to take everything so damn seriously?

    Why did I have to ruin all the good things in my life?

Why did I have to be so dogmatic, so joyless,
        so me?
What was stopping me from leaning in and kissing Tatiana
before the inevitable apocalypse
                (I'm sure I would have adored her lips)
or from telling Lensky that he was right
to believe in his dreams
                (or even from sharing those beliefs)?

Lensky.   If he was here now,
                it would make him laugh
to hear me soliloquising the way he used to do,
        simply,   plainly,   without frills,
and with a few swear words thrown in too . . .
Fuck, Lensky!
        If only I'd had your heart, your ambition . . .
how I wish
        you could have been a ventriloquist
and spoken through me to Tatiana so we might have kissed . . .
how I wish that you had laughed
        at all my colourless, closed-minded convictions
instead of always being in thrall
to everything I said, and imagining that I, this loveless lout,
was the one who knew what he was talking about . . .

oh, the two of you, idiot savants,

why did you believe all my rants?

*****

ME   Not bad. Sounds almost like Lensky. So you can
        be lyrical when you try . . .

EUGENE I guess it comes with age.

        But listen, I need your help.

        What should I do? What should I say?

        Should I tell her about all my regrets?

        Tell her that I've changed, deep inside myself?

ME   I'm sorry, my dear, but I think

        that bird has flown.

        She has changed too, you know.

        She and I are very different, it's true,

        but I understand her point of view:

        the life you're offering her is not

        what she wants.

        She's found her own way in life, without you.

EUGENE But I love her!

ME   And she loves you too.

EUGENE Really? How do you know?

ME   What can I tell you?

I'm psychologically astute
about things like that, and besides,
I feel like I've heard a story a bit like yours
once or twice before.
EUGENE What should I tell her?
ME   'Tatiana, I'm so sorry.
          I've been an idiot – will you please forgive me?'
          Start like that.

                    Tatiana, i'm so sorry
          i've been an idiot – will you please forgive me?

listen, there's no point in getting into all this
i'm not angry
the way you rejected me still chills me, even today,
but you didn't act badly
you could have taken advantage of me, and you didn't
in a way you were quite gentlemanly
i ought to thank you

                    no no please don't thank me
                    i was wrong! i know it now
          Tatiana i have to see you somehow

Silence.

No little pencil.

The silence goes on so long

      that for a moment

           Eugene thinks he's been abandoned.

And then she starts to write again:

if you want we can meet for coffee before i leave
the day after tomorrow i'm free in the morning
my flight is at 5 a.m.
p.m. I mean

                                      no

The pencil shivers.

Erases, then scribbles

again.

ok then never mind

                            can I see you now?

asks Eugene.

Blank.

310

no

Blank.
Pencil. Pencil.

i can't right now
i'm at the library

> *which one?*
> *the National?*

no at sainte geneviève
i'm really busy i've got a deadline to meet
i'm free in the morning the day after tomorrow
take it or leave it

Eugene's telephone turned orange.   Which meant
                                                 Absent.

*****

Tatiana slammed her MacBook shut,
opened it again,   closed it,
          ope . . .   no, just halfway,
                                        shut it, and then

thought about opening it once again . . .

      calm down, sweetie, it's a computer, not a fan

      or an accordion.

      So . . . back to work?

              no? oh, you're going home?

I don't know. Leave me alone.

    But you can't leave yet –

    you haven't finished taking notes.

who the hell are you,

my thesis supervisor?

                  no

then leave me the hell alone

         ooh I see, a little touchy . . .

  well, it was kind of a disaster, that conversation, wasn't it.

        What exactly did you hope to get from it?

I don't need your

hang on, don't forget

    your library card.

    Are you upset?

      Do you want to talk about it?

      Not just yet?

Poor, poor Tatiana.

Her face aflame,

she looked   adolescent,
even more   than she did   ten years before,
     if you can imagine that;
what I mean is that, although her face had grown,
of course,
not only in size, but in beauty and elegance,
     yet it was possible to detect, beneath its refined features,
     flashes of maroon and purple like the blushes
     that flush across the skin of octopuses
     and other sensitive sea creatures;
     you know as well as I do how it feels
     to have those sudden hot red weals
     spread across your face, this blaze
     that time extinguishes, but can never quite erase ...
oh God he screws me up

Oh dear, here we go again.
Skype and long-lost loves don't mix.
He turns my life upside down, he devastates me.
Hardly a surprise – I always knew it.
From the day we first met, my fate
was sealed; I was bewitched.

                    Hey, me too!

What do you know?

I should have realised that I would never
be able to rid myself of him – ever

Same for me.

He sticks to me like glue, and because of him,
I stick to the kid I used to be,
when I was young and naïve,
a pathetic little nothing . . .
I really was nothing back in those days.

You're hard on yourself.
Maybe it failed back then; maybe you were
small and weak, but not anymore.
Maybe now you're big enough to do something great.
Look how filled he is with remorse
and regret. It could work this time, I bet.

No. We were always fated
to pass each other by.
Back then I was passionate
and he was apathetic;
he never even thought of tomorrow while I
wanted all of eternity.
Now I feel that the opposite is true.
He needs someone in his life, and I don't.

Yeah, right.

What?

Nothing, sorry. Go on with what you were saying . . .

I want to be free, so this would never work at all.

I don't want to end up like Olga, with her love so banal.

Eugene's the one stuck in a rut now;

he's changed his life story;

truth is, we've always had opposing trajectories.

Okay, if you say so.

It's strange though,

because to me, it seems

like he's headed straight in your direction.

What do you mean?

He's on his way.

On his way?!

He's coming up Rue Soufflot

towards the library as we speak.

What? Right now?

Yep.

And he's entering . . . with an old library card,

which surprisingly has not expired.

How do you know?

I know everything.

He's climbing the staircase.

315

What are you going to do?

Pick up my stuff and go.

Then you'll bump into him
at the top of the stairs.

I'm trapped.
I'm trapped.
(She sighed.)   *Typical. I'm trapped*
just like I always was.

Oh give me a break – you're not some tragic heroine.
Go and talk to him.
You know, if I were you,
I'd cover him with kisses and hug him till he's blue.
Tatiana looked up at the lacy arches
of the library's ceiling,
perhaps searching for someone who could hide her,
but all the other students' heads were buried in their books,
multi-coloured earplugs shutting out the world,
a row of identical spiders
spinning webs of knowledge,
vacuum cleaners hoovering up philosophy
in handy bite-sized quotes,
perfect for college.
Go on, Tatiana,

the sole fly among all these arachnids,
unplug your ears and spread your little wings,
leave these nodding heads far behind . . .
go on, buzz off
and fly into his arms.
No one's paying any attention to you
(except me)
so let go of your qualms.

You poor deluded girl
(she says to me – can you believe her nerve?)
there's absolutely zero chance of that. We're not on TV.
Thankfully I have a little dignity.

Okay then.
At least I tried.
Go ahead, I'll watch you being dignified.

Tatiana met Eugene at the top of the stairs,
she holding her computer to her chest like the breastplate
of a knight,
he with eyes wide open, head spinning and light
after running all that way, climbing all those steps, dizzy
with the thought of all he still had to do,
and he, who I understand so well

(much better than Tatiana, in truth)

wanted to take her in his arms the moment they met

(and how I would have loved that, had she been me),

but she

whispered icily,

detaching herself from his embrace,

'Eugene,

I don't want to have a scene in this place.'

But why not?

It's the perfect backdrop,

this palace of paper and leather and stone,

with its extraneous extras exhibiting no emotion,

but already she was in motion,

hurtling down the stairs,

and he followed.

'Tatiana, I have to talk to you ...

listen to me, please!'

and his bass voice, thickened by the passion he felt,

echoed

down the stairway, bouncing off the walls,

and she slowed,

exhausted by this suddenly powerful voice,

his desperate pleas,

and on the staircase he managed to grasp her hand.

And when his fingers pressed
against her flesh,
                    it seemed to both of them that the steps
turned upside down, plunged and climbed,
                    abruptly,
                              and they saw
the library staircase
                    redesigned
                              by Escher,
                              and the only thing
that stopped them falling
                    was his hand
                              holding hers.
'Tatiana, listen,' breathed Eugene, 'listen to me,
                    this is all wrong. I mean,
I understand that your work is
                              important to you, and,
          you know, Caillebotte,
all that stuff, too,   but

listen ... I promise: never
                    would we ever
                              be bored together.
I swear it: I was off my head ten years ago; today,

everything is so utterly different.

If you stay with me here instead of going over there,

we'll be together forever like you wanted back then,

like I want now . . .

        listen

                listen to what I want . . .'

      And he told her what he wanted, in an undertone,

            while all around them swirled

            the flood of rushing students:

for Tatiana he enumerated

      the millions of billions of possibilities,

      a world of their own;

      for her, he narrated

the chapters of their life to come,

and he told them so sweetly, so softly, all those stories,

tales of epic journeys and secret caves,

      little details like their wet footprints at the

entrance to a Roman shower,

      breakfasts shared in bed, the tray of food sailing

on the duvet's waves

      in the striped Tuscan sunlight that pierced the

Venetian blinds.

      He described them all so sincerely and so wittily,

these joys both tiny and sublime:

the palazzos, the museums, the Chianti wines
(and yes, obviously he had a thing about Italy).

We can learn to ski together –
I've never tried.
You can watch me fall headfirst into the snow.
And one day I might take you on a surprise trip
to the Venice Biennale, and while you survey
the works on display,

I'll put my arms around you and nuzzle
your neck and stroke your hip.
One afternoon in Place Alphonse-Deville
we'll sit on the bench in the square
and read each other passages from books that we feel
are too special not to be spoken in the open air,
and then that night,
while the two of us are strolling hand in hand
we'll bump into a colleague on the street
'hey there how are you I'd like you to meet
my girlfriend Tatiana'   *and he'll see you*
and stand there stunned, so dazzled he's practically blind,
and I'll smile and say, 'sorry, mate, this one's mine'
and then

one day we'll meet your best friend
and I'll tell you afterwards 'wow she's pretty

and she seems like a really great person too'.
(whereas in truth she's nothing next to you)
just to see a little rush of jealousy
sting your face, so I can apologise and kiss it away
and
our bodies like eels in a bath of foam,
tedious meals at my parents' home,
the liquorice smell of your hair,
two glasses of white wine at the bar downstairs,
all of this and more will be ours . . .
coming home on the train
from a weekend away,
on my shoulder your tired head,
on my leg your slender wrist,
and sparkling there,
in the train's harsh light,
a little bracelet that I bought for you
to commemorate our first kiss
and all these moments, Tatiana,
when we'll be so close,
the two of us,
the hairs on my forearm pricked from static
after I roll up the sleeves of my jumper,
reaching out to touch the hairs on your forearm,

forewarned

that you are

   so near that I

     can turn my face

      a few inches

       to the left

        and your

         lips will

          brush

           mine

            and we'll

            thrill

to the touch
even though it happens every day,
even though it's normal,
our hands and thighs and hair and hips   *all touching*
         all the time ...

in air-conditioned airport lounges,
behind rain-streaked windows on creaking trams,
at tables in friends' houses as we eat dinner,

    while yawning in endless traffic jams
      (because even when we're bored,
      we won't be bored of each other –
      and at least we'll be together),

in hotel rooms where sheets and pillows
have been kicked to the floor and suitcases spill clothes,
in the cinema on a Saturday night

        in the flickering light
from the screen,

    in all these places where all I will have to do
in order to kiss you

    on your temple

       is lean down

          slightly,

   in all those moments when we lightly
     turn out the light.

And then ...

  And then, what?

  What else would Eugene have to do or say

  to Tatiana before she yielded to his passion?

  How could she say no after such a declaration?

Just to be on the safe side, he began a negotiation

  (let's not forget that he is Chief Business Adviser

for his company);

    attempting to sound tougher and wiser,

    he set out to demonstrate

    that there is always a solution.

'Tatiana, there is always a solution –

you know what,   I'll go with you
        screw my job, I don't care about that:
for you, I'd jump on the first plane to San Francisco
and live with you there, I'd make it my home …'

                                                    Gripped
by this vision, our Eugene starts making lists in his head
of all the things he'll do to make her happy:
I'll cook for her every day, and keep
the kitchen well equipped
with food and all that stuff,
and I'll massage her feet and her back and shoulders
                        long enough
                                to destress her after a hard day at work,
I'll accompany her to every exhibition,
                                        I'll read every article she writes,
                                        and if she ever feels down,
                                        say one November morning,
                                when the world is cold and ugly and brown,
                I'll arrange a miniature bouquet of mimosas
                in a shot glass for her
                and I'll put it on her bedside table before she wakes up,
                bright yellow, like a little bursting shrubbery of
Honey Loops,
and by its side

I'll leave a Post-it saying: 'hey lover,
I'll see you this evening –
and I hope everything goes well for you at the meeting.'
And perhaps Tatiana's mind was filled with similar ideas,

because she squeezed his hand tighter
and her eyes blurred with tears
and she

You know what?   I really think

that I can see her hesitate,   gesticulate,
stare at the floor,   stare at the stairs,
stare into Eugene's eyes   stare through the window outside,
stare into a future filled with all those moments,
as yet unlived,

stare at the prospect of those two Americas:
one towards which she sailed already,
loyal captain, compass steady –
that promised land
of a life she'd elected.
The other a continent unexpected,
in the way of her navigation:
Eugene,
and oh that way he affected
her body, her emotions:
here be dragons,

the map warned her;
no – no – we'll be – say it! –
we'll be bored together . . .
And, faced with these two directions,
Tatiana was in agony,
burning up, torn apart,
her poor heart
aflame,
while her brain
screamed in vain;
despite herself, she was in love . . .
IN LOVE!
again!

. . .

and yet
all the same
she was aware
that something was   not quite right here:
something was off,
a grain of sand between the gears,
a pea beneath her thick thick mattress
so tiny, and buried so deep,
but still . . .   enough to cause her some distress,
enough to disturb her peaceful sleep;

her conscience, like a thousand darts
pricking the pincushion of her heart,

       the certainty that this
       would not be happiness,
       this unsatisfactory compromise;

Eugene, so impassioned and adorable,
but Eugene also like the heavy ball

       attached to the chain around her ankle.

And her life – her own life – like a guilty pleasure,
a desire she could never completely meet . . .
Tatiana had a vision of those two passions, each defused;
she saw herself alone and together with Eugene,

       in an American living room, sprawled on a
gigantic sofa, staring at a huge TV screen,

       caressing each other sadly, their dreams dented,
bruised,
forgotten,
the two of them sunk in silence,
not wishing to blame the other
for an existence
that could have been
so much better . . .

                            'No.'

She said it.

I don't believe it.

She said no. She refused.

'No, it's impossible,

the time isn't right.

I don't know what else to tell you

except:

I'm sorry, and I have to go;

except:

this hurts me as much as it hurts you;

except:

of course I'll regret it, we both will;

but that's the way with everything, don't you see?

I'm sorry, Eugene,

I really do have to go.

I'm already not really here, you know.'

Eugene realised that she wouldn't surrender,

that she would leave him behind,

and he resigned

himself to this fate, almost as if . . .

. . . as if he'd felt the pea under his mattress too

and realised that even a thousand nights of making love,

pounding the pea down from above,

would not be enough

to make the bed smooth.
There was only one thing left to do,
one sole concession that he might tear
            from the hands of fate
before this love vanished forever,
one last resort before it was all over:

> Give me a night   or two.
> Give me the chance to show to you
>   what it is that I mean when I speak
>   of my love;
>   and then I'll bow out. Enough.
>   Unless you ask for more.

And taken with this thought he heard himself implore,
            'You know, it's not too late:
we still have two days,'   he whispered,
'when we could be together . . .'
This thought made his whole body tremble with desire
        and he caught hold
        of Tatiana's cold
        white tense hands
        and
        he said
please.   This was his only reality now,
this breathless vow,

and she, in his eyes, was radiant

with hesitation ...

please

please please

please please please please

please please please please

please please please please please

please please

please please please please

please please please pl

please ple

ase please please

please please please please ple

please please please please pl

ease please please please please

please please please please ple

please please please

please please please please ple

ase please please please plea

please please please please pl

ease please please ple

please please   please plea

se ple

ase ple

ase ple

ase pl

ease

please

please

no but

why not

but   why   not

not no but why

no   but   why   not

no   but but why

not   no   but why

not no but   why not

why not no but   why

but   why not no

no but why

no but why not but

not no but why

not   no   but   why not

no but why not

but why not no

no but   why

not no but why

not   no   but

why not no but

why not

no but

why

no

but

but

why not

Tatiana murmured,
'Eugene, it wouldn't be worth the suffering –
two days is nothing.'

                      'No, two days is better than nothing;
                two days is so much; it's a glory, it's a prize;
              go tell a butterfly that two days is nothing.
                  Two days is twice as long as the
                        butterfly lives before it dies.'
And suddenly,

                              I remember –

I remember a story about a butterfly,
and the fleeting vision of a fine dark line of hairs –

                    *****

Oh I believe that it was that fleeting vision that saved
            Eugene and Tatiana this time,
            because ten, a hundred, a thousand times before,
at this point in the story, she'd have run away,
                  she'd have left the library,
she'd have passed through the curtain of light and
disappeared,
just as Eugene feared;

and he would have been left alone,
the diamond of his happiness turned to sand
escaping between his fingers,
stunned at having held it in his hands
so tightly, only to see it slip away,
and he'd have knelt on those twisted stairs,
collapsed in despair,
and on a final, deafening note,
we would all have wept with him
       (yes, even I,
        and I hardly ever cry) . . .
we would have wept for the Tatiana
he had lost forever,
      for the vast void at the centre
      of his life and,
         in the centre of that centre,
         another empty space:
         Lensky
and Olga and the huge tiny nothingness of his life;
we would have wept
for these Russian dolls all taken apart,
all emptied of their hearts.

But this time, things are different.

Because this time, there is this memory,
this sudden flash of lust,
this arrow loosed from the depths of adolescence,
and personally, I have absolute trust
in the power of such a remote reminiscence
and all the others that it trails in its wake;
I believe they are capable of changing the course
of a story,
even a story written and played
and played again so many times,
even a story that we know by heart,
even a story barricaded by the masters of their art
in a famous opera, a long poem;
and it seems to me –
I believe this truly –
that when we are confronted by the past,
even accidentally,
when we are brought suddenly
ten thousand feelings
back in time,
then this padlocked poem, deathless,
perfect, so fine,
thick with the dust of two hundred years,
can be made to change its final lines.

And so,

at that moment, as if swift fingertips
were reaching through the distance
of centuries to place between Tatiana's lips
a blueberry, ripe with the taste of her teenage past –
the taste of that summer so tragic and sublime,
the taste of nights spent watching the stars
spark and die,
imagining embracing and being embraced,
wondering which path she should take –
and if, when lying next to Eugene,
she would have known
how to touch, caress and taste,
then at that moment, ten years on,
when all her dreams
suddenly acquired the blueness and roundness of the real,
Tatiana opened her lips

to

reveal:

'Two days, and that's all.'
'That's all,'

replied Eugene,
immediately swearing to himself

that all would be everything.
Everything: every possible rectification.
Everything: every possible justification.
Everything: every wrong righted, every sin redeemed.
Everything: the endless night of lovemaking he'd dreamed.
Everything: all their greatest and their least desires,
and everything:

> every pleasure and every fear
> hoarded over the last ten years,
> over the last two hundred years,
> theirs, of course, but also yours and mine,
> and those of the whole wide world,
> all of them, compressed into an attic bedroom
> in the ninth arrondissement,

> > behind the Grévin Museum;
> > everything: the two of them

among the waxwork figures,
so that when they came to the end of their life
they could say:

> those two days were everything;
> those two days were so full of love;
> those two days   were enough.

Everything: and from the moment when
on the staircase

transformed to a snail's shell all around them,

      a perfect spiral, a sinuous helix,

      Tatiana finally brushed her lips against the skin

      of Eugene's neck,

      at the very edge of his jumper's collar,

      pulling it back

      like the taut entrance of a tent . . .

                          from the moment

when he lost himself in her hair and the voices in his head

began to sing,

      they lived through

                 absolutely

                        everything.

                 *****

I'm not going to draw you a picture.

It's not as if I watched . . .

      well, not much,

      I hardly saw anything really,

      just a glimpse between the curtains,

      but still . . .

           you know, dear reader,

or you will,   those explorations,

                              those treasures,
those pleasures,   those elations,
those comings and goings,   those speedings and slowings,
      those thousand astonishing tiny details,
                    those kisses like stones skimmed across the sea
                                   of our bodies,
            those melodies
modulated ever more exactly, as their fingers learn to know
the tone of each key beneath their touch,
            the softening or sustaining of the pedals;
and I know that you know – that you will know –
where to find,
            in the most hidden nooks and crannies,
            all those funny secret little handles;
and so it was that they liberated scores of shivers,
            like birds released from cages unsuspected
                    with keys and keyholes unexpected,
and they followed their flights upwards to the skies
                    with wondrous sighs,
noting the ideal weight to be pressed and time to be waited,
taking it in turns to be locksmith and liberated;
            they entered those new uncharted lands,
            clumsy and solemn as children,
                    discovering

those sudden little folds of skin

that are instrumental,

releasing the music of clarinet

or violin.

And you know perfectly well what I mean when I say
that it was beautiful

the next morning,

that exhausted light of six a.m.,

and that it was a glorious day outside in the din

of the binmen's lorries,

forcing them awake, and then –

since it was impossible to say no –

picking up what they'd let go

barely a few hours ago,

crumpled in the creases of their sheets:

their love.

You know all that,

I trust you do.   And so

Tatiana and Eugene,

during those forty-eight hours of bliss,

broke the evil spell of adolescence,

rediscovering its delights without its defiance,

and that is what I wish for myself

and it's what I wish for you too, darling

reader: that we will perhaps experience
this everything:
a love
like a nectarine, as perfect, round and smooth,
a love
that can be held in both hands and can soothe
the tremors in your soul,
a love that is whole:
the love that Eugene and Tatiana shared –
unbridled, uninhibited, unembarrassed,
unique and universal –
for those two days in his single bed
in that attic room in Paris.

8

And with that, my task is done.
I am rid of them.
I promise

that they will be happy
for at least two days.

And afterwards?
I should warn you,
I can't promise that two years from now,
when she returns from California,
they will leap into each other's arms . . .

although you never know.

I want to believe so, for I do have a heart.

But I can't swear to anything.
Because, it seems to me, and this can't be ignored,
that a love like theirs is perfect for two days.
After that, however,
we'd probably all
get a little bit bored together:

you and me, maybe,
of the two of them;
the two of them, perhaps,
of each other.

Acknowledgements

The French version of this novel already contains a million mercis, so I won't repeat those here. To any potential readers of both versions: they still stand. And actually, if you are a reader of both versions . . . well, thank YOU. My goodness. You are my favourite kind of geek.

I could not, obviously, begin without thanking Sam. His translation – which I prefer to call a version – is a work of unbelievable wit, creativity, audacity and charm. Reading the first full draft of Sam's translation was doubtlessly one of the most wonderful and uncanny experiences of my writing life so far, and working with him over the next few months was exhilarating, intellectually and artistically rewarding, frustrating at times and above all really a lot of fun. Alors merci, Sam. Je suis devant ta traduction comme une poule qui a trouvé un couteau.

Huge, huge thanks to Kirsty McLachlan and to Phi-Anh Nguyen for selling the rights to Faber. I'm grateful beyond words and still amazed that this particular text made it beyond the French borders. And Faber picked it because Leah Thaxton and Camille Morard managed to convince everyone. I know how tortuous the route into British translation can be, and I can never thank them enough.

I am so grateful to the whole Faber team, who have been relentlessly supportive and passionate about the book from the very first Skype call to the first bound proofs. Emma Cheshire and Lizzie Bishop went well beyond the call of duty promoting it to foreign publishers – thank you so, so much; thank you especially also to Hannah Love – like Eugene and Tatiana, we meet again! – and to Natasha Brown, whose wonderful calm, humour and attention to detail made such a difference to the whole process. Very many thanks, too, to the Wednesday Books team, who are so enthusiastically taking care of the American version.

I am extremely grateful and honoured that James Fenton let us use the title of his poem as the title of this book and the lines for the epigraph. I must admit that Baudelaire didn't get asked about the French version.

Tibo Bérard, my French editor, was the original midwife; Alice Swan and Sara Goodman's editorial work gave birth to this English version. Thank you, thank you, thank you to the three of you for believing in this text so much, and for your wise, patient and creative work on it.